Advanced Praise for
Life on Christmas Eve

"A powerful story of love and grace wrapped in a festive, nostalgic tale." —Bob Goff, *New York Times* bestselling author of *Love Does* and *Dream Big*

LIFE on CHRISTMAS EVE

a novel

NATHAN NIPPER

Post Hill PRESS

A POST HILL PRESS BOOK
ISBN: 978-1-64293-920-0
ISBN (eBook): 978-1-64293-921-7

Life on Christmas Eve:
A Novel
© 2021 by Nathan Nipper
All Rights Reserved

Post Hill Press
New York • Nashville
posthillpress.com

Published in the United States of America

1 2 3 4 5 6 7 8 9 10

For Finley Faith - my dream daughter.

Chapter 1

As Julie discovered, Christmas Eve in her hometown of Cedar Springs was an ideal time to do something odd in a public setting. With most folks preoccupied with family celebrations at home, the likelihood of one's curious behavior garnering notice, let alone being questioned, drastically diminished. Julie counted on the streets being mostly deserted after dark because she could not adequately explain her current enterprise: sitting by herself in a collapsible camping chair at one end of the small town's iconic steel truss bridge.

It was 6:05 p.m., and snow descended in weighty clumps from the starless, black-matted sky. Julie knew she looked bizarre wrapped in a sleeping bag and blankets, a thermos of hot cocoa at her feet, like she was waiting for a parade to start or camping out in line for concert tickets. She felt entirely self-conscious and was the first to question her own sanity. She also felt inexplicably compelled to be there at that very moment, though the compulsion was not quite strong enough to chase away her potential embarrassment.

As a few cars traversed the narrow two-lane bridge at a leisurely holiday pace, Julie tried burrowing deeper into the canvas seat of her camping chair, as if it might help conceal her from the glow of the headlight beams. Some motorists noticed her; others did not, or at least pretended not to. She was rather hard to miss in her prominent seated position on the sidewalk that ran alongside the decades-old bridge railing. One car slowed as it approached, and she tensed with fear the driver would stop to ask questions. It was not an unfounded fear. Julie loved her salt-of-the-earth fellow Cedar Springs citizens, but one less desirable common trait in the community was a tendency toward nosiness. Sometimes a gal just wanted to be left well enough alone. And there was never a greater such instance than the one in which she placed herself that evening. Julie instantly prepared a contingent reply to any inquiries. She would say she was "just enjoying the snow," or something similarly lame, which would be truthful without divulging the actual reason for her visit to the bridge. She made a snap decision to smile and wave enthusiastically at the craned-neck driver, figuring that might better discourage questioning than if she sat motionless, hoping not to be noticed. Fortunately, the car continued on its way.

Julie did not want to be interrogated because no rational explanation existed for why she sat by herself on the bridge in the freezing Christmas Eve air. The truth was that she was waiting for something to happen. She had no idea *what*, just the most persistent hunch it would be something *important*. The only similarly strong intuition she recalled having in her life was the time in fifth grade when she was almost certain she was going to get a full-size backyard trampoline for Christmas. Alas, no trampoline materialized.

Just as she was about to laugh off her intuition incompetence and rejoin the sane world, something *did* happen.

While Julie contemplated packing up her solo bridge-watch party, she began dozing. With the hot cocoa, the abundance of fleecy layers, and the soothing lull of the icy river cascading over the boulders directly below the bridge, her surroundings soon faded into a wintry fog. She resisted the first couple of head-bobs but quickly gave up the fight and drifted off.

Julie was only asleep for a couple of minutes when a violent, metallic clatter jolted her awake, her left leg involuntarily flailing in the process. Her eyes fluttered open and she brushed the wet snowflakes from her face. She leaned forward in her chair, momentarily disoriented, and surprised to realize she had fallen asleep. Glancing cautiously back and forth, she hoped no further passersby had witnessed her conked out on the bridge like that, as it would be impossible to explain her way out of that one.

Having regained her bearings, she peered straight ahead, squinting through the thickly falling snow across the bridge. She could make out a dingy blue and white pickup truck with its right front fender crumpled against the dense trunk of a majestic cedar tree, one of several such trees just off the shoulder of the road near the start of the bridge.

Julie stood, trying to gather her senses and find her phone. She checked her coat pockets, the camping chair, and the snow-caked concrete around her to no avail. *Perfect*, she thought, figuring she left it at home. The unscathed driver's side door of the crashed pickup truck slowly opened with a rusty, drawn-out squeal, interrupting Julie's annoyance at forgetting her phone. As she watched, a haggard teenage girl tumbled out of the cab and fell to her knees in the snow. She lingered on the bitter cold ground for a moment, weeping loud enough for Julie to hear. The girl picked herself up and stumbled alongside the guardrail for several yards until she stepped onto the sidewalk of the bridge. Julie froze at the alarming scene unfolding in slow motion. In her sleepy stupor, Julie could not settle fast enough on the best course of action.

Oblivious to Julie's presence, the girl's deep, sorrowful crying persisted as she trudged aimlessly through the ankle-deep snow of the bridge's sidewalk. Julie noted the girl wore only a sweatshirt and jeans, which had to be scant protection against the night's biting cold. The teen stopped near the middle of the bridge and leaned over the railing, prompting Julie to shift forward uneasily in her chair. Beneath the bridge, the churning dark river surged over and around large, smooth boulders on its way toward the falls. The girl's shoulders convulsed with her breathless sobs. From Julie's vantage point, she assumed the girl must be feeling sick.

Julie looked around, suddenly hoping for a crowd. But the streets were empty and quiet, as if the town was taking a deep breath, finally about to allow itself a respite from all the frenetic Christmas preparations. Julie and the teenage girl remained the only two souls on the bridge.

Finally, Julie's habitual compassion overruled her hesitation. With a deep breath of her own, she stood, unfurled herself from the blankets, unzipped her sleeping bag, and piled them on the camping chair. Then, she cautiously approached the grieving stranger. Between the din of the rushing river and her own weeping, the girl did not hear the crunch of snow underfoot as Julie crossed the bridge toward her...

Chapter 2

Julie's descent into bridge-stalking could be traced back four and a half weeks to Thanksgiving Day. She blamed leftovers and the movie *It's a Wonderful Life*.

Julie's alarm woke her at six o'clock on Thanksgiving morning. She always set her alarm to WPVS, the small town's only radio station, where Cal Stevens was the primary DJ. They had gone to high school together, though he was a couple of grades ahead of her. When Julie's alarm sounded, Cal was in the middle of a mini-monologue about the dearth of Thanksgiving-specific songs, and how, because of that, he liked to use the occasion to kick off the Christmas season. Thus, Andy Williams's *It's the Most Wonderful Time of the Year* dutifully ensued. As much as she loved the Christmas season, Julie did not necessarily concur with Cal's choice. She felt one should at least wait until Friday to roll out Christmas tunes, since Thanksgiving was continually swamped in the ever-growing Christmas tidal wave.

Julie's respect for Thanksgiving resulted from her parents' cultivation. They prioritized celebrating Thanksgiving with the warmth, gratitude, and sincerity it was designed for. That is why she did not mind dragging herself out of bed at 6:00 a.m. on one of her few days off—that plus the fact they had to finish preparing Thanksgiving dinner for fifty guests from the local nursing home.

Julie Shelly was thirty-one years old. She had dark brown eyes and hair that her mother had always reassured her was "a lovely chestnut," but which Julie labeled "bland brown" or worse. She usually wore her hair in a hastily assembled ponytail, less out of any stylistic statement and more out of pragmatism. She worked at her family's bakery-café, which meant she rose at 4:30 a.m. every weekday and did not budget hair-coiffing time into her minimalist morning routine.

She was five feet, eight inches tall, with a slightly athletic build that she often lamented had been in perpetual decline since her graduation from college. She hypothesized that with each additional year of life beyond age twenty-two, regular exercise became exponentially more difficult to maintain. This nominal fact did not sit well with her. Another lamentable fact of life was her fair complexion. She was sure her mother single-handedly kept sunscreen makers in business during the summers of Julie's youth, considering the gallons lovingly slathered on her daughter each time she ventured outdoors.

Julie threw on her gray wool coat, which she had owned for at least a decade, as the holes in the pocket interiors attested. She wrapped a red wool scarf around her neck and exited the small apartment where she lived over her parents' detached garage. It was a cozy flat with recessed lighting, one bedroom, a bathroom, and a combination living room/kitchenette. It looked like something out of an IKEA catalog because that was where she purchased most of the furnishings. It took her several years of parental loans and savings acrobatics to do so, but the end result was worth it, no matter how many Swedish jokes resulted, courtesy of her dad and older brother, Hugh.

The reason Julie resided in the space over the garage, even though she could have her old bedroom in her parents' photogenic Victorian house, was as a result of a brief but intense rebellious period during her junior year of high school. She craved independence at the time, accusing her parents of having given Hugh much more liberty during his high school sojourn than they afforded her. Though it embarrassed her to recall it now, she stubbornly made an issue out of it to the point that she threatened to go live with friends (even though, secretly, she had no viable offers on the table). Her dad's patience-of-Job conflict resolution was to let her help him finish out the garage apartment, a project on which he had been tinkering for years. If she put in the work, she could be the apartment's first and only tenant. She leapt at the chance, and by the end of the summer before her senior year, the father-daughter combo fashioned a livable space. Though it pained her mom to see Julie move out of the house and across the driveway into the garage apartment, she knew it was decidedly better than the alternative.

The garage apartment solution had the desired effect on seventeen-year-old Julie, creating some semblance of separation and independence. She continued living there after high school graduation, commuting to the University of North Carolina at Asheville over the next six years while working nearly full-time at the family's bakery-café. Ironically, though Julie craved separation as an angst-ridden teen, she was still living in the garage apartment at thirty-one. Her original plan was to leave Cedar Springs when she finished her college degree six years ago. But seasons change, plans alter, and before she knew it, her thirty-first birthday was in the rearview mirror.

Julie descended the flight of stairs from her apartment and quietly unlocked the side door to her parents' house, which opened into the laundry room. She slipped into the kitchen and set two cards in envelopes on either side of the small breakfast nook table where her parents began each day with their bibles and coffee. Julie was a dedicated card person. When she was in college, she began making her own cards of all types—holidays, birthdays, graduations, thank-yous—and it blossomed into a minor hobby. People seemed to appreciate the personal touch she put into her cards, and that was her favorite part—making people feel special with a card they wouldn't find in any store. The cards she left on the table for her parents were relatively simple ones, letting them know how thankful she was for them. They were already aware of this fact, but she enjoyed reminding them anyway.

Light snow fluttered in the air as Julie walked the half-mile into downtown Cedar Springs. She did not always walk to work but decided the first snowfall of the year was too invigorating an occasion to miss with a car ride. It was unusual to see snow that early on the calendar in Cedar Springs, and she loved it. The colder the weather, the merrier as far as she was concerned, as the holiday season would not be the same without coats, scarves, and hot drinks. She could not fathom how Floridians coped at Christmastime.

Cedar Springs, North Carolina, population 7,203, was unabashedly quaint. It seemed designed for Christmas cards with its old-fashioned globe streetlamps, churches with steeples, picket fences, and manicured Main Street storefronts. An arched, steel truss bridge that was painted a warm red stretched over a narrow off-shoot of the French Broad River that flowed into a gorge on the edge of downtown. The town was a tourist trap in the best sense of the words. It thrived on tourist expenditures without the stereotypical gaudiness. Through the decades, the town's savvy zoning kept most chain restaurants and mass retailers on the northern edge of the city limits, preserving the historic buildings and local businesses of downtown. Cedar Springs was perfectly situated as a gateway town to the Blue Ridge Mountains of western North Carolina, so vacationers funneled through the tidy village in a spending mood. This enabled many downtown small businesses, shops, and eateries to thrive where they often would not have in most similar-sized towns. Though Julie frequently felt restless and fatigued with the familiar small-town culture, deep down she knew Cedar Springs was an idyllic place to make a decent living, and it was the only place she had ever called home.

The Shelly family's slice of the Cedar Springs economic pie was Shelly's Boulangerie & Café, a bakery and coffee establishment founded by Julie's late grandfather in 1946. The family often referred to it as the "SB&C," while most of the towns-folk simply called it "Shelly's." Julie had worked there over half her life—part-time starting when she was fourteen, mostly full-time since she was nineteen. She barely knew what it was like to sleep past 4:30 a.m. anymore, which was the very latest she could wake up and still make it to the SB&C by 5:00, to help ensure everything was shipshape for opening at 7:00 a.m. sharp. For Julie, waking at six o'clock on Thanksgiving felt luxurious.

Julie turned left off the Main Street sidewalk, striding around to the rear of the SB&C. She unlocked the back door,

which led into the kitchen. She switched on the lights and began warming the ovens. From there, she entered the café proper, turning on additional lights and igniting the gas fire in the
brick fireplace situated on the back wall of the dining area. The
SB&C's interior featured the original exposed brick walls, dark
hardwood floors, rustic oak tables and chairs, a long pastry case,
cappuccino machines, and two casual sitting areas with couches
and overstuffed chairs. The cozy ambience was a beloved gathering place for Cedar Springs citizens of all stripes. Farmers in
overalls and hipsters in AirPods felt equally at home at Shelly's.

By 6:30 a.m., Julie's parents, Bev and Perry, and her aunt,
Bonnie, arrived at the café, accelerating the Thanksgiving feast
preparation. Bev and Perry both turned sixty-five in September,
though their spry energy made them seem a decade younger.
They still walked or rode their bicycles nearly every day, just
as they had for all forty years of their marriage (they seemed
to be exceptions to Julie's adult exercise hypothesis). Their un-
wavering devotions in life were their Christian faith, each other,
their family, laughter, and work, in that order. These comprised
their base formula for a rich, contented life. It was not effortless,
though Julie thought they mostly made it look so. Julie admired
them and envied their vitality. She often felt guilty on many dark
winter mornings when it required every muscle fiber in her body
to pry herself from her bed. Only to arrive at the bakery to find
her dad already there, his blue eyes bright with life, a smile on
his gently wrinkled face, his silver hair impeccably coiffed, tall
and strong in his khaki slacks and crisp button-down Oxford.
His sleeves would be precisely rolled up to the elbows, his apron

already dusted in flour, toiling away as if he'd been up for hours. Her mom was no less a vision of neatness, efficiency, and positivity. Bev was petite, especially when standing near the six-foot-five Perry. She had light brown eyes and gray hair, worn in the same short style she'd adopted at least twenty years ago by Julie's accounting.

Some may have found their polished attire rather formal for their line of work, but Perry always insisted quality began with appearance. When Julie was a brooding teenager, her dad's fastidious mantra sometimes annoyed her, like when she would be asked to clean a minor kitchen mess or wipe down tables that she did not think required attention. But she eventually grew to understand why you did not leave any crumbs on the counter, or underneath the tables, or smudges on the glass of the pastry case. Appearance *did* matter, and she was convinced her dad's attention to detail was a vital ingredient in the family's recipe for business success.

Bev and Perry made a unique team, swirling about the bakery with the synchronization of an ice-dancing pair. Julie sometimes scrambled to keep up with them, but she grew to admire their consistency, which made it hard to grumble on those days when she longed to hit the snooze button. If her parents could still run the family business with such gusto when many folks their age were checking into retirement villages, who was she to complain? She occasionally joked about wishing she shared her parents' genes; however, she was adopted. Not that she was remotely forlorn about the fact. She was barely four months old when Bev and Perry took her in from the North Carolina state foster care system. The Shellys *were* her definitive family. In fact, she rarely pondered being adopted. Through the years, she felt occasional pangs of curiosity about her biological parents, but never enough to make her attempt to find them. And why would she? Surely none could surpass the Shellys in the wealth of love they heaped on their daughter.

Promptly at eleven o'clock that morning, two white vans, each with *Cedar Springs Nursing Home* in black lettering on the sides, parked alongside the curb as close as possible to the SB&C entrance. Above the doorway to the café hung the original metal sign, designed and painted by Julie's grandfather, which read: *Shelly's Boulangerie & Café, Est. 1946.*

Julie bounded out the front door, greeting the van drivers and assisting with the lengthy process of disembarking the senior citizens, several of them in wheelchairs, and carefully escorting them inside the warm café. Julie was proficient in patience with the seniors, including a warm hug for each lady and gentleman and an attentive ear to several lengthy chats. Most of them knew her by name, and their faces lit up as she greeted them individually. To those she did not know, she eagerly introduced herself and they eagerly reciprocated. That was the trend with Julie— she seemed to leave a trail of brightness wherever she went. She first had the idea of hosting the nursing home guests for Thanksgiving dinner when she was in college. Now in its ninth year, the dinner was a bona fide tradition for the Shelly family.

Julie and Bev moved expertly among the elderly guests, seating them at neatly prepared tables with turkey and cornucopia centerpieces. Once all the guests were situated, Perry stepped out from the kitchen wearing his standard SB&C apron over a white dress shirt and a sharp red tie for the special occasion. He held up both hands in his gentle, unassuming fashion to gain the diners' attention, then asked their permission to give thanks.

"Heavenly Father, we thank you for your generosity of provision and for the company of these dear friends," said Perry. "Thank you for our nation and the freedom we enjoy. We thank you for this food and for your sustaining grace. Most of all, we thank you for your unfailing love and forgiveness. In the name of Jesus Christ our Lord, amen."

A slight grin lingered on Julie's lips at the conclusion of her dad's prayer. She loved the rather formal manner in which he prayed.

Perry shook hands with the nursing home chaperones and drivers before joining Julie, Bev, and Bonnie, who were already circulating among the tables, serving steaming plates of Thanksgiving fare. The eyes of the elderly guests twinkled with delight as Julie addressed them, listened to them, and put her arms around them. Several gratefully patted her arm as she assisted with cutting turkey on their plates and refilling their beverages.

✳ ✳ ✳

It was nearly two o'clock in the afternoon by the time the leisurely meal concluded, the tables were cleared, and each guest was safely back onboard the nursing home vans. Julie craved a nap back in the cozy quiet of her apartment. Instead, she walked a few blocks north of Main Street to the Cedar Springs Community Church, where she had one more Thanksgiving commitment to keep.

She entered the church's large, all-purpose meeting hall where folding tables and chairs were scattered about and the din of jovial conversation permeated the air. Sixty-year-old pastor Tim Duval, his wife Maggie, and several members of the congregation had just finished serving Thanksgiving dinner to a group of twenty-three Congolese refugees. The refugees fled their war-torn homeland a year earlier and the church members took them in. The group was temporarily housed, fed, and clothed in the church's annex gym for the first couple of weeks until units in a local apartment complex became available.

Julie had been a member of Cedar Springs Community Church for as long as she could remember. At ten years old she walked the aisle, made her profession of faith in Christ, and was baptized by Pastor Tim. Post-high school, Julie was more sporadic in her church attendance than her parents, or even Aunt Bonnie. To her parents' credit, they never pressured Julie about church. The reasons behind her spotty attendance were complex and difficult for her to articulate. It ultimately came down to the fact that Julie, though she unreservedly considered herself a Christian, found life's perplexing gray areas a constant challenge to her faith. She related more to Thomas, Jesus's disciple famous for his doubt, than to an apostle like John. She often found herself praying the words related in the gospel of Mark, when a man said to Jesus, *"Lord, I do believe; help me overcome my unbelief!"* That encapsulated her faith.

She had more questions than answers, so she sometimes found it difficult to relate to the platitudes and seemingly undoubting faith of fellow parishioners. She often felt like an outlier Christian, wrestling with doubts and deep theological questions that her church community either glossed over or were unwilling to address.

Another more practical explanation for her uneven worship participation, however, was that the SB&C closed on Sundays, which was usually her only day of the week to sleep in.

Despite Julie's doubting-Thomas tendencies, she was always eager to serve in various capacities in the church. She was the first person called to substitute in the nursery or for children's Sunday school classes, and she frequently pitched in for church youth group events. The church, and the wider Cedar Springs community, were familiar with her genuine compassion and reliability. She was first in line to help out when the church decided to care for the twenty-three Congolese refugees. There were four Congolese families in all, with fifteen children among them, aged two to fourteen. The children adored Julie, which is why she committed to stopping by that afternoon to read them her favorite Thanksgiving picture book.

The children cackled with delight at Julie's enthusiastic rendition of *The Pardoned Turkey*. When she finished the short book, the children applauded as if at a Broadway show. Pastor Tim and his wife Maggie stood outside the ring of children and eagerly joined in the applause. Julie closed the book and stood from her metal folding chair, prompting the crowd to swarm her for hugs, and she obliged each one individually.

Van Beal entered the meeting hall with a soccer ball under his arm. Following close behind him was a gaggle of teenagers, four girls and two boys, all regulars in the church's youth group. Thirty-one-year-old Van was six feet tall, with a boyish face and gait. He had friendly brown eyes and auburn hair, which was frequently covered with a baseball cap. For this occasion, he wore a red knit beanie with a *Cedar Springs High School Soccer* emblem embroidered on the front. He was an English teacher at the town's high school, where he also coached varsity boys' soccer and the coed tennis team.

Julie noticed Van's arrival, smiled, and waved at him.

"Who's ready for soccer?" shouted Van. "Sorry, *football*," he corrected himself for the kids' amusement. His words barely hung in the air before the children cheered and swarmed him, snatching at the ball. Van teasingly kept the ball out of their reach, prompting several to jump on his back, trying to bring him down. Van winked at Julie, and she shook her head in amusement.

Behind the church lay a well-worn field with patchy grass, surrounded by a chain-link fence. Each end of the field had small soccer goals with chipped white paint and rips in their weathered orange nets. A chaotic soccer match ensued between hodgepodge teams of Congolese children and the church's youth group teens. As Julie good-naturedly played goalkeeper for her side, she shoved her hands deep in her coat pockets, her teeth chattering against the frigid wind. Light snow continued falling, adding to the inch that already coated the field.

Van stood in the opposite goal, though he ventured many more ridiculous dribbling forays than Julie ever thought of attempting during the raucous pickup game. She chuckled at Van's antics with the kids. He was a lovable goof and a close friend. It was surprising, particularly to the older ladies of the church, that some fortunate young woman had yet to snag him. Bev had even suggested Van as a match for Julie on a couple of occasions, with Julie dismissing the notion as utterly ridiculous.

Julie was single, with no serious boyfriends in her past and no serious current prospects. While she was interested in getting married and starting a family someday, she was not desperate, and there was a big difference between the two, as she occasionally had to remind her matchmaking Aunt Bonnie. To be certain, a slight sense of panic occasionally washed over her when she lay awake at night pondering the fact she was thirty-one years old and lived in a small town where the shelves were relatively bare in the husband department. But she was also mindful that marriage was not a trifling venture and therefore justified in her pickiness.

Though her remaining in Cedar Springs and working at the family business seemed to indicate otherwise, Julie was uninterested in settling. She had a more sophisticated theoretical husband in mind, whom she generally assumed she would meet after she made her escape from Cedar Springs. She envisioned meeting this soul mate in a place like Oxford, perhaps in one of C.S. Lewis's old haunts, where they would certainly get lost in endless discussion of books, theology, and ideas over countless cups of hot tea, falling madly in love in the process. He would speak with a pleasant British accent, wear smart tweed jackets without hipster pretension, and be all-around delightful.

One of the refugee children, a six-year-old girl named Marie, slammed the ball past Julie into the back of the net, snapping Julie from her Oxford reverie. The girl ran away, arms raised in celebration. Another one of the Congolese children, an eight-year-old boy named David, let a snowball fly that smashed into Julie's shoulder. She feigned outrage and set out for revenge. In short order, the soccer match devolved into a free-for-all snowball fight, with Van providing expert instruction on snowball construction to the uninitiated Africans on his side of the field. One of the youngest boys complained of the frosty sting on his bare palms as he tried to fashion his own snowball. Julie overheard Van assuring the boy that the pain was temporary, but the glory of a compact snowball properly connecting with one's foe lasts forever. Van frequently made absurdist asides like that for his own amusement—it was simply one of the ways he enjoyed life.

Once several kids collapsed on their backs in the snow from snowball fight exhaustion, Julie lay down beside them and demonstrated how to make snow angels. Soon, a host of snow angels of all sizes regaled the entire field.

By dusk, the Congolese families began dispersing for home. Julie said goodbye to everyone and politely declined an offer from Van to drive her home. The snow had stopped falling and Julie felt a leisurely stroll through the brisk air back to the SB&C would be a satisfying way to cap her frenetic, yet fulfilling, Thanksgiving Day.

Back inside the café, Julie worked on stringing white Christmas lights in the front windows. The following day would signal the start of the Christmas season, and hanging a few lights was a relatively easy way for her to get a jump on the café's decorative transformation. As she worked, a police cruiser stopped and parked across the street from Shelly's. A female officer, thirty-two-year-old Beth Bishop, got out of the vehicle and walked the short distance across the street toward the SB&C.

Beth was slightly taller than Julie, with a similar, mostly trim build, which made it convenient for them to borrow the occasional item of clothing from each other as needs arose. Beth had straight black hair and olive skin she inherited from the Cherokee ancestors on her dad's side. Julie first met Beth in seventh grade when Beth's family moved to Cedar Springs from South Carolina. They became almost instant friends and had been inseparable ever since.

Beth waved at Julie through the window and Julie hurried over to the front entrance to unlock the door, letting her friend escape the cold.

"Hey!" greeted Julie.

"Happy Thanksgiving!"

"You want any leftovers? I was just about to pack up some and bring them to you." Julie stepped back onto the short ladder to finish hanging one last strand of Christmas lights.

"Are you kidding?" replied Beth. "Of course! I'm starving."

"Well, I knew you both had to work today, and we had tons of food, so…"

Beth's thirty-three-year-old husband, Eric, hustled inside the café wearing a short-sleeve fire station t-shirt tucked into khaki work pants. He was tall and lean, with brown eyes that matched the color of his stubble beard.

"What is up, ladies?" he asked, shivering from the cold.

"Babe, where's your coat?" asked Beth.

"Left it in the truck."

"Looks like you won't have to take me to *Denny's* after all," said Beth. "Julie needs help with all her leftovers."

"Thank God," replied Eric in mock relief. He was a head taller than Beth and leaned over to kiss her. "I guess this makes Julie awesome or something."

Julie grinned. That was Eric—perpetual humorist and sarcasm expert.

"So, what are you up to tonight?" inquired Beth. "Why don't you come over and help us eat your food?"

"No, it's okay," said Julie stepping down from the ladder and admiring her lighting handiwork. "I'm not hungry. The ladies at church put all kinds of pie pressure on me. I totally caved."

"Nothing wrong with pie pressure," said Eric.

"You don't have to eat to come over. We were going to watch *It's a Wonderful Life*," added Beth hopefully.

"Eh…I'm really tired. I'll probably just go home. I have to get up extra early in the morning for the Black Friday crazy people rush."

"Come on, party pooper," said Beth, gently tugging on Julie's arm. "Who tries to resist *It's a Wonderful Life*?"

"Actually, I've still never seen it," confessed Julie with a slight wince.

"What?" said Beth, looking slightly offended.

"Really."

"That's embarrassing," said Eric. "And basically communist."

Julie narrowed her eyes at Eric.

"Seriously, how have you not seen *It's a Wonderful Life*?" inquired Beth. "I mean, I know you're not much of a movie person, but…"

"Yeah, and I just can't really get into black and white movies."

"That's one of the most ridiculous things I've heard you say. Which is saying something," said Eric.

"That settles it then," said Beth. "We can't let this go any longer. You're coming with us."

Julie protested weakly, "Did you hear me mention how tired I am?"

Julie finally relented to Beth's invitation. She gathered the Thanksgiving dinner leftovers into a large picnic basket, while Beth left to park her cruiser at the police station. From there, Eric and Beth swung by the café in his truck to pick up Julie, and the trio made the short, meandering drive north of downtown to their small, three-bedroom brick house.

✳ ✳ ✳

Initially, Julie tried to pay attention to *It's a Wonderful Life* just to be polite. The opening scene of an apparent conversation amongst angels in heaven, peculiarly conveyed onscreen by pulsating, talking stars, did little to dissuade her prejudice against "old" black and white movies. But then, she was surprised by the early shift in tone when a mourning, drunken pharmacist, Mr. Gower, slaps young George Bailey's damaged ear until it bleeds, punishing the lad for apparently not delivering a prescription to Mrs. Blaine like he was supposed to. The heart-wrenching drama of the moment seized Julie's full attention. Then, when Mr. Gower discovers the truth that George actually prevented poisonous pills from getting delivered, a lump formed in Julie's throat, and she was caught off guard by stinging tears in her eyes. She reached for a tissue on the lamp table beside her chair and glanced at Beth who grinned at her as if to say, "*I totally knew this movie would get to you.*"

The rest of the classic film gripped and charmed Julie quite unexpectedly.

Beth and Eric shared the couch with their feet up. Beth worked on her second piece of pumpkin pie while Eric fell asleep. By the film's climax, when George Bailey's war-hero brother, Harry, toasts his big brother and the townsfolk serenade George and Mary with *Auld Lang Syne*, tears trickled down Julie's cheeks. She was startled and slightly embarrassed by her emotional gush. Between bites of pumpkin pie, Beth nonchalantly passed Julie the box of tissues.

"*Told* you," remarked Beth as Julie gently blew her nose and dabbed her eyes.

Eric stirred awake in time to notice Julie's tearful state and asked, "Why's she crying?"

"You know, 'cause George is the richest man in town," replied Beth, who might have been similarly affected had she not already seen the movie umpteen times.

"Oh," he said, disinterested, nestling further into the couch and closing his eyes again.

Julie barely noticed their calloused reaction as she pondered how she had possibly managed to miss this movie her entire life.

Chapter 3

The morning after Thanksgiving became busier each year for Shelly's Boulangerie & Café. Whether it was shoppers staying local in Cedar Springs or pausing for breakfast on their way to the mega retail center fracas closer to Asheville, the patronage tide always swelled at Shelly's on Black Friday morning.

As Bev made final preparations at the main counter for the expected onslaught, Perry entered from the kitchen, peering out the windows at the giddy crowd waiting on the sidewalk outside the front entrance.

"Christmas shoppers! Let the holidays begin," he declared cheerily. "Seems like we just did this. How does every year get shorter?"

Perry paused on his way back into the kitchen to kiss Bev on the cheek. Julie exited the kitchen in time to glimpse Perry's marital affection and Bev's appreciative grin. Her parents had been affectionate that way her entire life. There was a time during her tween years that the kisses and hugs grossed her out. But the older she got and the more cranky married couples she observed, she appreciated that her parents had the rare marriage. She had a growing concern, particularly now that she had crossed the thirty-year-old threshold, that she would be unable to find a husband who could live up to the kind of compatibility, warmth, and love her parents shared. With no time to dwell on the matter in the moment, she brushed it aside to haunt her another day.

"I've never liked that it's called 'Black Friday.' It doesn't sound very holiday-ish," remarked Bev out of the blue.

"I'm with you, Mom. It sounds too stock market crash-y."

A series of strong electronic pings caused Julie and Bev to glance around, and at each other, confused. Just then, Bonnie breezed in with a tray of chocolate croissants for the pastry case. As she opened the case, the ping sounds grew louder.

"There it is!" exclaimed Bonnie. She pulled her smartphone from the pastry case. "I finally figured out how to set reminders on this contraption. But I keep losing it. And then, when I find it, I forget to type in the new reminders for the day. It's a very vicious cycle."

Bonnie was Perry's younger sister. She was sixty-three years old but had the short-term memory of a person thirty years older. Bonnie had a healthy sense of humor about her weak memory, just as she did about most things in life. Like Perry, she had lively blue eyes and well-worn laugh creases on her friendly face. She was slightly shorter than Julie, pleasantly plump, and unselfconsciously pear-shaped. She was rarely seen without wearing a hat of some sort, usually of the stocking variety. Her ever-present headwear seemed like a subconscious effort to keep thoughts, memories, and general information from escaping her brain (if that was indeed the hats' purpose, they failed miserably). In spite of her forgetfulness, Bonnie somehow had a perfect recall of pie recipes. Pies were her specialty and one of the SB&C's signature offerings. Apple, chocolate, pumpkin, pecan—if something could be made in pie form, Bonnie's version was the best.

Bonnie checked her frequently missing phone. "Okay, two minutes to showtime."

Julie maneuvered around Bonnie and Bev toward the entrance. "Close enough," she said, flipping the Open/Closed sign to the "Open" side and unlocking the door. The bell over the door jingled as a middle-aged couple stepped inside as the first customers of the day.

"Hey, another angel got its wings," said the bubbly wife to her unsuspecting husband.

"Huh?" replied the husband, missing her reference. The menu board already preoccupied him.

"That's funny," said Julie, overhearing the wife, "I just watched that movie for the first time last night!"

"Really? Oh, it's my all-time favorite!" replied the woman. "I watch it every year."

"Yeah, I really loved it. I can't believe I'd never seen it before."

"My husband still hasn't seen it either. Every year I try to get him to watch it with me, but he won't."

"Watch what?" said the husband.

"*It's a Wonderful Life!*"

"Oh, that. Yeah, I don't like black and white movies."

The wife rolled her eyes toward Julie, who smiled knowingly.

An old classmate of Julie's named Sandy Wilson squeezed inside the already-bustling café. Sandy sparkled from head to toe in the trendiest kind of "casual" Fall fashion that, pricewise, was anything but. She had perfect hair, a perfect designer handbag, and perfect furry winter boots. She looked like a million bucks for a good reason, as she was actually worth at least twice that.

"Julie! Hey!" said Sandy, maneuvering her way through the crowd toward the counter.

Julie glanced over her shoulder from the cappuccino machine. "Wow, Sandy Wilson! How are you?"

"Fantastic! How 'bout yourself?"

"Good, you know. Crazy busy." Julie winced on the inside
for having stated the obvious. She regretted the subconscious
need she always felt to impress Sandy Wilson. She stepped to the
counter with a coffee in each hand for waiting customers. "How
long have you been in town?"

"Just got here Wednesday night. Couldn't pass up the
chance for a Shelly's muffin, of course." Sandy pointed to a large
pumpkin-chocolate-chip muffin in the case. "But I'm heading
back to Nashville tomorrow."

Julie pulled the muffin from the case, put it in a small
SB&C-labeled paper sack, and handed it to Sandy with a smile.
"Business is booming, I hear."

"It's *insane*. We're opening stores in three more states
next quarter."

"That's amazing!"

"I know! Baby clothes—who knew?"

"Well, I guess it's a pretty *fertile* market." Julie felt rather
pleased with herself for conjuring that one so quickly.

"Ha! I'm totally going to use that. So, what about you?
Made it around the world yet?"

"Not quite."

"I figured you'd already circled the globe several times
by now."

"No, but I actually have a plane ticket now. I'm leaving
New Year's Day."

"Oh, yeah? Where to?"

"London first. Then the rest of Europe, then South Africa, Japan, Australia, New Zealand. I'm going around the world like Nellie Bly. Except I'm taking my time."

"That sounds *unbelievable!*" replied Sandy as she handed Julie a twenty-dollar bill for the muffin.

Julie stepped over to the cash register and made change from the bill, enjoying how it felt to finally have a grand-sounding, tangible plan to announce—especially to someone like Sandy, who practically invented grand, tangible plans. It was not that Julie begrudged Sandy any of her wealth and success. Sandy certainly was not arrogant about her status. It was just that being around her dredged up all of Julie's inadequate feelings. Chief among them was her seeming inability to ever leave Cedar Springs and finally commence her dream of seeing the world and writing books about her adventures.

"Good for you, Jules. You deserve it." Sandy was the only person, besides Van, who sometimes called her *Jules*, something Sandy started when they were in middle school. Julie handed Sandy her change, all of which Sandy promptly dumped in the tip jar on the counter. "Okay, gotta run. Black Friday deals beckon. That's what's so great about the rag biz; I can write off all my shopping as research." Sandy winked and turned toward the door. "Oh, hey, when do the big Shelly lights kick off this year?"

"December first. Our seventieth year!"

Harriet Paddock, an endlessly scowling seventy-two-year-old, hobbled inside the café just in time to overhear Julie's pronouncement. Harriet quickly interjected with a smirk, "I wouldn't count on that just yet!"

Sandy shot a quick look of sympathy toward Julie. Virtually everyone from Cedar Springs knew of Harriet Paddock, and no one liked to interact with her. Harriet was reputed to be the wealthiest citizen in the county. She was also quite possibly the stingiest and most irritable. Very few people knew much about her anymore, as she led an increasingly hermit-like existence. However, she still resided in what was considered a mansion by Cedar Springs standards, on a two hundred-acre spread just beyond the western edge of the town, where she had lived alone for decades. She seemed to emerge only when there was something to gripe about. But when she went to the trouble to do so, she made her presence felt to all around her. Van once remarked that Harriet was "Twitter in human form," a description Julie found remarkably accurate.

Harriet was a large woman, vertically (six-feet tall) *and* horizontally (exact weight unknown, but ample). She walked with a limp, aided by a cane, due to her bad knees. Her limp, combined with her girth, turned her walk into more of an angry stomp, which was a fitting outward extension of her general enmity for humanity. She had perpetually flushed jowls, framed by stringy, shoulder-length gray hair that she clipped back with a single barrette on her right side. She did not bother trying when it came to personal appearance, and she resented anyone who did. Most Cedar Springs folks were rather intimidated by Harriet. She relished the fact and burnished that reputation at every opportunity.

"Take care, Sandy!" said Julie, waving bye before mustering her best patience and shifting her attention to Harriet. "Good morning, Ms. Paddock. How are you today?" Julie forced herself to smile.

Harriet used her cane to step closer to the counter and slapped down an envelope in front of Julie. "You don't have to pretend to care with me, young lady. If your first thought when you see me coming is '*crap, here comes that old hag,*' then just say *that*. Or don't say anything. Just don't be fake. Veiled contempt is *still* contempt. And it really doesn't become you."

Harriet's gruffness was a toxic agent on Julie's bright holiday mood. It also jarred Julie's ability to control her tongue.

"Thanks for the tip, Harriet. I would say it doesn't become you either, but I've never seen you display anything *other* than contempt, so…" She secretly regretted already losing her cool with Harriet. However, she reasoned Harriet would surely try the patience of even the Lord himself.

"Okay, smart-ass, where's your dad?" demanded Harriet, her right hand still clamped over the envelope on the countertop. A few customers standing at the pastry case glanced sideways at the irksome woman, and Julie was pretty sure she noticed them shift further away.

Perry entered from the kitchen seemingly on cue. The immediate sight of Harriet at the counter dimmed his smile somewhat, though he tried to conceal it. "Ms. Paddock!" he began. The Shellys usually aimed high with Harriet by starting with the formal *Ms. Paddock*, though the polite tone could rarely be sustained very long with her. "Can I get you a cup of coffee? Perhaps a croissant?"

Julie stifled a smirk as only she could detect the sarcasm seeping from her dad's friendly offer.

"Nope." Harriet slid the envelope across the counter to Perry. "Consider yourself *served*."

Perry glanced skeptically at the envelope without picking it up. "Beg your pardon?"

"I will be acting as my own attorney, so I'll see you in court. I wouldn't finish unraveling those lights quite yet." Harriet shook a crooked finger at Perry and managed to twist her scowl into a slight grin before turning back toward the exit. Customers shuffled swiftly out of Harriet's way, as if proximity to her anti-Christmas aura might infect them.

Perry sighed, his brow suddenly wrinkled with weary concern. He waited until Harriet exited the café to open the envelope and reluctantly examine the documents inside.

"What is it this year?" asked Julie.

"She's suing to shut down the Christmas lights."

"Again? Shocking development."

"Looks like she's getting creative this time. 'Public nuisance' lawsuit. Let's see...." his eyes raced over the pages, "Apparently, the traffic causes her 'undue mental stress and anxiety attacks.'"

"*Public nuisance?*" interjected Julie. "Isn't anything that messes with Harriet Paddock more of a public *service?*"

Perry's furrowed brow temporarily softened, and he chuckled at Julie's wry observation. "I'm getting too old to deal with this." He sighed again as concern returned to his face.

Julie put her arm across her dad's shoulders. "This too shall pass, Dad. It always does. Some guy used to tell me that all the time."

Perry grinned at her, but even as she said it, Julie could not help the creeping doubt that this year was different. The Shellys were accustomed to Harriet's effort to halt their popular annual Christmas lights display in downtown Cedar Springs—she had tried suing twice before. But Harriet seemed unusually confident that morning and Julie hated that her dad would once again have to waste time and money during the holiday season, traipsing to court to deal with Harriet's vindictive pestering.

Even as they discussed Harriet's latest lawsuit, dozens of volunteers from the town were hard at work piecing together and hanging the elaborate "Shelly Family Christmas Lights Spectacular," which stretched the entire length of Main Street. Julie and her parents joined the volunteer teams whenever they could work around their busy SB&C schedule. Volunteers had already been assembling the display for a week, and it would take another week to have it ready in time for the traditional December 1st opening night.

The Shelly Christmas lights display began in 1948 when Perry's parents, Hope and James, paid for (out of their own meager SB&C profits from that year) strands of lights and a Christmas tree to decorate the courthouse square in downtown Cedar Springs. They were inspired to do so by their mutual love of the Rockefeller Plaza tree in New York City, which they saw for the very first time together shortly after meeting in 1942.

Theirs was a typical wartime whirlwind romance. They met at a G.I. Christmas party dance. Hope was a Navy nurse, James an Army Air Corps paratrooper. When they left the dance, they took a long walk together, ending up at Rockefeller Plaza, where there were three smaller Christmas trees that year—one decorated in red, one in white, one in blue—rather than the customary single grand tree. They sat in the plaza and talked for hours, in spite of the cold.

They courted ever so briefly before separately embarking overseas, she to North Africa and he to southern England. They wrote weekly letters for the remainder of the war. In James's last letter before parachuting into Normandy on D-Day, he proposed marriage. The anticipation of her reply kept him going through the army's grueling two-month slog toward Paris. Finally, with the Eiffel Tower visible on the horizon, he received a letter from Hope with her answer: *absolutely yes.*

James celebrated Hope's acceptance of his proposal by treating himself to a pain-au-chocolat and a café au lait in a Parisian boulangerie. He sat outside the bakery, reading her "yes" letter over and over until he had it memorized. That experience became his inspiration for the name of the future "Shelly's Boulangerie & Café."

James almost made it to war's end unscathed, but just a week before Germany's surrender, a land mine ravaged his left arm, shoulder, and neck. He never had full use of his arm again. Once he was released from a British hospital and shipped stateside, Hope met him in Cedar Springs, where they were finally married in December 1945. They scrimped and borrowed to start Shelly's Boulangerie & Café, which opened the following spring. They poured their lives into the business, rarely missing a day of work and rarely taking vacations, until they both died of natural causes, within three months of each other, in 1999.

The Shellys' modest lights display grew exponentially through the decades, becoming a beloved Cedar Springs tradition, with the town's citizens eagerly volunteering to help construct and take down the display each season. By the time Julie was in junior high school, the lights had become a small sensation in the region, with people even driving from Tennessee, Virginia, and South Carolina to experience the town's charming holiday brilliance. There were even occasional stories about it on local TV news stations in Raleigh-Durham and Charlotte. Everyone in Cedar Springs seemed to love the lights. Everyone except Harriet Paddock.

Chapter 4

By noon, the Black Friday rush at the SB&C slowed to a crawl, so Julie took the opportunity for a break and walked a few blocks west to Cedar Springs Camera Supply. She loved the old store, which came of age when film development was a large part of its business and managed to stay afloat when film faded away by converting to the digital camera age. It also catered to tourists by selling framed prints of regional scenery, taken by local photographers, including a few by Julie. She was a minor photo hobbyist and hoped to become a more proficient photographer during her epic trip abroad.

Few people knew of her desire to one day write a travel blog featuring her own photographs and essays about her exotic globe-trotting adventures. She did not talk about it much because she was shy about the outlandishness of her dream. Since her parents and grandparents had spent their entire lives doing the same thing in the same place, she felt a little black-sheepish about wanting to do something completely outside the family business. Sure, Hugh had gone off into the Coast Guard, but at least that was serving the nation. She was also shy about her dream because she knew it was rather unoriginal, with at least half the world's population also pining to write a successful travel blog that enabled them to make a living as a world traveler. She knew the odds were ridiculously stacked against her, but she continued to nurture the dream anyway, albeit mostly in secret.

Her most recent stab at legitimacy was writing a lengthy article about off-the-beaten-path places to visit in her region of the Blue Ridge Mountains. Six months earlier, she submitted the article, purely on spec, to *Travel+Leisure* magazine. She was more crushed than she would like to admit when she never heard back from them.

Inside the camera shop, Julie took aim with the digital camera she had been eyeing for weeks, examining its features and toying with the lens. Jim, the balding, middle-aged shop owner, grinned across the counter from her.

"This is the one, Jim. You'd have to work hard *not* to get amazing shots with this."

"True," replied Jim, patiently. He was accustomed to Julie's periodic lunch-break camera-dream sessions. It was one of the ways she stoked the embers of her globe-trotting ambition through the years.

"We're meant to be together. I've felt it for a long time. I've just been saving so much for my trip. It's kind of hard to spring for a new camera when my old one still works, you know? Especially if it means two less weeks in New Zealand."

"Okay. So, go ahead and book those weeks then."

"What do you mean?" asked Julie, still gingerly holding the camera.

"You want me to box it up? Or do you want to wear it out of the store with the carrying strap and case that I'm throwing in?"

"Jim...do *not* tease me now. What are you talking about?"

"I'm talking about you getting acquainted with your brand-new camera."

"What, are you running a free camera Black Friday special or something?"

"Well, I'm sworn to secrecy, but apparently someone bought you an early Christmas present. My instructions were to let you keep whichever camera you picked out next time you came in the store."

Julie's mind raced, trying to figure out who was to blame for this ludicrous generosity. *Mom and Dad? Aunt Bonnie? Beth? Surely not Sandy Wilson, though she could afford it more easily than anyone she knew.*

"Okay, who was it?"

"Don't even try. My lips are sealed."

"No way! It's too much. Tell whoever did this, thanks, but I can't accept."

Jim pulled a piece of paper from his shirt pocket, unfolded it, and read the note aloud: "'If she tries to say she can't accept, just place the camera around her neck and force her out of the store.' Come on, Julie, don't make me forcefully remove you."

She leaned across the counter, trying to glimpse the note, but Jim quickly refolded it, stashed it in his front pants pocket, and grinned satisfactorily at her.

Julie shook her head and continued looking over the camera in disbelief. As she did, Van breezed into the shop, peering closely at a couple framed photos hanging on the wall to the right of the front entrance.

"Wow, Jim," said Van, "you'll let anyone sell photos in here if they pester you enough, huh?"

Julie looked over her shoulder at Van. "Those are *mine*, dork."

"Oh, hey, Julie! Didn't see you there," he teased. He looked closely at another framed photo as if noticing it for the first time—a photo of the red Cedar Springs steel truss bridge in springtime. "This one's not too bad, I guess."

She playfully glared at Van as he joined her at the counter. He waited patiently as Jim attached the neck strap to Julie's new camera, then handed her the box and carrying case. She thanked Jim profusely for his indulgence, then left the shop with Van.

"Notice anything different about me?" She modeled the new camera around her neck, also highlighting the leather carrying case strapped over her shoulder.

"Wait, don't tell me…new haircut?" asked Van. "That's usually what women mean when they ask that, right?"

"I just got probably *the* best Christmas present ever! And I don't even know who to thank. Well, I have a couple of parental suspects, but how awesome is this?"

"Does this mean we'll get to see some decent photography from you for a change?"

She grinned sarcastically. "*Some* people will."

"Look at you, all ready to take on the world. *Julie versus Wild*—I'd watch that show."

"Now I can't tell if you're mocking me, or…"

"For real."

"Thanks then. It's nice for a change."

"What do you mean 'for a change?'"

They continued the friendly banter on the short walk back to the SB&C. Van followed Julie inside to get a cup of coffee. As usual, she tried to keep him from paying for it by utilizing her go-to joke that he needed to save his meager teacher/coach's salary. As usual, he paid for his coffee anyway by stuffing his money in the tip jar when she was not looking.

"Did you get all your Christmas shopping done today?" she asked.

"Nah, I'm more of a Cyber Monday shopper myself. You know, less crowd-fighting."

"Sure. Makes sense. So, you've got it all planned out, huh?"

"I'm actually more of a Christmas Eve afternoon shopper. Now *that* will get the adrenaline pumping."

She shook her head, chuckling. "I could never do that."

Julie tried out her new camera by snapping a few shots of Van and his coffee cup while he feigned annoyance.

"You going to the big fundraiser Tuesday night?" he asked.

"Don't think I've missed one since they started, so, yes."

"Well, I didn't want to presume," he replied.

"I'm helping out with the silent auction."

"Anything good this year?"

"I don't know, guess you'll have to show up and find out," she answered while scrolling through the photos on the camera's display.

"I was planning on it."

"Good."

"Maybe I'll see you there."

"Maybe so."

"Good," he said, taking another sip of his coffee while she snapped another photo of him. Aunt Bonnie strolled past them, carrying empty mugs on her way to the kitchen. Julie caught her aunt's mischievous grin and playful eye roll, though their precise meaning was lost on Julie.

Chapter 5

The following Tuesday evening, Julie entered her parents' house through the laundry room, breezed through the kitchen, and into the dining room, where she found her mom and dad eating dinner. In her rush, she grabbed a piece of the sliced baguette on the table, glancing at her parents' tired faces and noticing they seemed quieter than usual. "Did I leave my coat in here?" she asked on her way to the living room.

"Want me to get you a plate?" Bev finally called after her.

"No thanks," replied Julie from the living room, "I'm about to be late for the fundraiser." She reappeared at the table, having found her wool coat on the living room sofa. She looked at her dad who slumped slightly in his chair and rubbed his forehead. "Are y'all not going?"

"Probably not. Your dad's not feeling well," replied Bev.

"What's wrong, Dad?" asked Julie between bites of bread.

"Just really tired. And thinking about this ridiculous lawsuit."

"I'm sorry. Well, it's only Harriet, right? I'm sure the judge will throw it out again."

"Maybe. But we did just elect a new judge, so who knows? And Harriet is relentless. She won't stop until she gets her way and they rename the town after her or something. It's preposterous. I don't have the energy to fight her anymore. I don't know. I was just telling your mom, maybe it's time to call it quits."

Julie looked at him with alarm. "What are you saying? We can't shut down the lights!"

"Well...I know. It's not what I *want* to do, of course. But a person like Harriet doesn't have anything better to do with her time and money. I can't compete with that. Seems like she wants to have this battle every Christmas now."

"We've got the whole town on our side, Dad. She'll lose again. She's gotta give up eventually." Julie stepped closer to kiss his cheek. "Don't worry about it. Hope you feel better."

"Have fun, dear."

Julie kissed her mom's cheek as well.

"Be careful!" added Bev, just as she had admonished Julie every time she left the house for as long as Julie could remember. Julie moved briskly through the kitchen and out the back door, sliding on her coat as she went.

❋ ❋ ❋

Julie drove her gray 2004 Toyota Corolla just a mile and a half north of downtown to Cedar Springs High School. While most of Julie's acquaintances from high school had long since graduated to newer, fancier vehicles, Julie still drove the same car her parents gave her as a high school graduation present. It was slightly used when they gave it to her in 2005, so it was now relatively ancient in car years. Julie could have replaced it a long time ago with something more substantial, but she was singular about saving for her trip around the world and therefore made do with her aging wheels. She usually felt a bit humiliated driving to public events in the old car with its chipped paint, one missing hubcap, and assortment of random noises. But she quickly brushed aside the embarrassment with the comforting knowledge that every monthly car payment she did not have represented another few days she would get to spend on her foreign adventure.

Julie parked as near as she could to the back entrance of the high school gym and unloaded two substantial gift baskets from the back seat of her car. The baskets overflowed with baked goods, coffee, and tea from the SB&C, which her mother and Bonnie helped her prepare earlier that afternoon. She lugged the dense baskets inside the gym, where the party atmosphere and dancing had just begun. She wove her way through the crowd to the performance stage, which filled the width of one end of the gym, and walked up the stage steps where a female volunteer helped her arrange the baskets among the myriad auction items.

An enormous painted mural covered much of the back wall of the stage, flanked by two giant artificial Christmas trees, one on each end. The high school's art students had painted the mural on long panels of butcher paper, which featured a man, apparently representing George Bailey, standing at the railing of the bridge in the memorable scene from *It's a Wonderful Life*. In the water below the bridge, the students depicted another man, apparently Clarence the angel, wearing a hat with his arms stretched overhead as if he were flailing in the water. Julie took in the mural and grinned, enjoying the fact that just a few days ago she would not have understood the painting whatsoever.

Draped above the stage was a long banner which read: *It's a Wonderful Life*...and underneath, *Lighthouse Adoption Network*, followed by *#GivingTuesday*. Julie read the banner, then noticed the woman helping with the auction items wore a 1940s-style dress and hat. Julie remarked to the woman she had not realized the fundraiser was a sort of costume party this year. The woman assured Julie a period costume certainly was not required and that Julie looked terrific. Julie was not underdressed, wearing a knee-length dress and sweater with boots—all rather formal attire (by her standards) that she rarely had occasion to wear. But as she surveyed the townsfolk milling about the gym and dance floor, she felt decidedly out of place. Most of them seemed to be dressed, if not as specific characters from *It's a Wonderful Life*, then at least as citizens of the 1940s.

Julie had attended the Lighthouse Adoption Network benefit events since they began when she was in junior high. Though the nature and theme of the event changed from year to year, it never featured a theme quite like this before. A jazz quartet played Christmas swing music for the couples on the dance floor. There was a "Photo with Clarence" booth where Julie's old high school science teacher, Mr. Laywell, was dressed in a dark over-coat and fedora like Clarence from the movie. Another area of the gym floor was made to look like the iced-over pond in which George Bailey's younger brother fell through the ice. Kids took turns sitting on scooter boards, sliding down a short plywood "snow" hill, then gliding along the gym floor and crashing into a barrier of white foam bricks. That was a particularly popular attraction among the youth in attendance.

As usual, Cal Stevens, the DJ and all-around voice of the town's radio station, served as master of ceremonies. There was a menagerie of contests, instrumental soloists, singers, dramatic readings, and skits, primarily performed by students from the Cedar Springs High School Fine Arts program. Cal effortless-ly transitioned between the performances and announcements concerning the silent auction, raffles, games, and booths. Cal's costume choice amused Julie. He sat in a wheelchair dressed as Mr. Potter from *It's a Wonderful Life*, complete with a dark suit and bald cap.

Pastor Tim and his wife, Maggie, entered the gym near where Julie stood and greeted her with hugs. They were not in costume either, which made Julie feel a little less out of place. As they marveled aloud about the benefit's décor and festive atmosphere, Robert and Susan Mitchell, who founded and ran the Lighthouse Adoption Network, approached dressed as George and Mary Bailey from one of the iconic scenes in *It's a Wonderful Life*. Robert wore a baggy old football uniform, while Susan wore a bathrobe, à la Mary, during the scene in which George inquires whether Mary would like him to "lasso" the moon.

"Mr. and Mrs. Mitchell! Love the costumes!" exclaimed Julie.

"What? This old thing?" replied Susan jokingly. "You're sweet."

"Thank you so much for donating the gift baskets," said Robert.

"Of course. It's our pleasure," said Julie. "We wouldn't miss it! How's it going so far?"

"It's going great!" replied Robert. He held up a small bell and added, "Hopefully about to get even better!"

"Right!" said Julie with a wink.

The jazz music faded to an end, the dancers on the gym floor paused, and Cal introduced "the founder of the Lighthouse Adoption Network." The crowd applauded enthusiastically as Robert Mitchell replaced Cal behind the microphone. He briefly recounted the humble beginnings of the charity and explained its purpose of providing financial aid to families who wish to adopt children. "Each one of the angel figures you see hanging from the rafters tonight bears the name of one child who has been adopted with the help of the Lighthouse Network. Since we started thirty-five years ago, that number has grown to over one *thousand* children."

The crowd erupted in applause and cheers as people looked up and around, astonished by the number of colored paper angel cutouts dangling from long strings. Julie smiled as she absorbed the inspiring sight, wondering whether one of the angel cutouts bore her name.

Robert briefly rang a small bell. "Now, thanks to Zuzu Bailey, we all know what happens when you hear a bell ring," he continued, "but tonight, whenever you hear this bell ring..." He shook the bell again for good measure. "It means we've reached another thousand dollars in donations! And remember, thanks to many extremely generous donors and church partnerships over the years, all our administrative costs are covered, so every cent of your donation tonight goes directly to help families adopt!"

Again, the crowd cheered and applauded.

"Thank you so very much for your generosity and support," continued Robert. "We hope you have a *wonderful* time this evening!"

The jazz quartet launched into a new musical set and the dancing resumed. Julie excused herself from Tim and Maggie to get a cup of hot apple cider from the refreshment table. She had one sip before Van arrived alongside her and scooped up a cup of his own.

"Good evening, Miss Shelly. And wow! Looking sharp!"

Julie glanced at Van as she took another sip. He actually wore a tie and blazer, quite the upgrade from his usual tracksuit look. He was, however, still wearing sneakers.

"Thank you. So are you. I almost didn't recognize you without your coaching hat. Nice jacket," replied Julie.

"Just a little something I threw together at the last minute. Okay, it's the only jacket I own. So, why aren't you dressed as a *Wonderful Life* character?""

She shrugged. "I guess I didn't really know the characters well enough."

"What?" Van looked incredulous.

"Well, I just saw the movie for the first time the other night."

"Seriously? What's your deal?" he asked with playful disbelief.

"I know. I'm lame. You know what's really weird, though? Since I watched it, it seems to be popping up everywhere."

"Is that right?" mused Van.

"Yes. Ever had that happen? Where you read or watch something or hear a song, and then stuff related to it starts randomly popping up?"

"You mean like déjà vu?"

"Not at all."

They laughed. Van drained his cup and turned to the cider bowl to dip a second serving. "I heard ol' battle-axe Harriet is trying to shut down the lights again," he said.

"Well, you know, it's a holiday tradition now."

"What a pain for y'all, though."

"Yeah. It's really hard on my dad. Seems to be bothering him more this time. I don't know, sometimes I almost feel sorry for Harriet. I can't imagine being so alone."

"But she definitely seems to bring it on herself." He glanced hesitantly at Julie, took a deep breath, and cleared his throat. "So, I guess I was thinking about dancing, possibly, at some point…"

Julie did not fully hear him as she was distracted by some-one she glimpsed on the opposite side of the gym. She craned her neck for a better look at the man. "Oh my gosh, is that Mike Hughes?" she exclaimed.

"I don't know," replied Van, looking much less interested.

"It is!" said Julie, dropping her unfinished cup in a nearby trash bin and starting across the gym floor toward Mike Hughes.

Mike finished chatting with a woman who walked away just in time for him to notice Julie headed his way. A grin quickly spread on his face.

"Mike?" asked Julie with a little hesitation.

"I'm sorry, do I know you?" teased Mike.

"Yeah. Julie?" She was pretty sure he was joking, but a tinge of doubt lingered as it had been a few years since they last saw each other.

"Well, yeah, I remember a Julie Shelly, but she didn't look this amazing," said Mike.

He stepped toward her and they hugged.

"What are you doing here?" asked Julie, still rather shocked to see him.

"I live here now."

"What?" Julie was genuinely confused. *He lived in Cedar Springs without her knowledge?*

"Yeah, I moved my practice here last month. My mom was still here, so she lives with us now. I just decided I wanted my kids to experience small town life."

Mike was a lawyer. Julie remembered the last time they saw each other he was studying for the bar exam, which she thought sounded dreadful—both the studying *and* the test.

"How are your kids?"

"Well, there are four of them now," he said, holding up four emphatic fingers.

"Four? How on Earth have you…"

He interjected, "Managed four kids since Karen died?"

"I wasn't sure how to put it, but…" Julie chided herself for indirectly broaching the subject of Mike's late wife—a tragic instance of a beloved, radiant woman stricken with brain cancer three years earlier.

"That's one of the main reasons we moved back here, so Mom could live with us full-time. I wouldn't have survived without her."

"I'm so glad things are looking up," said Julie, sincerely meaning it but hoping she did not sound flippant.

The music transitioned to a slower song, and Mike's eyes met Julie's for a long enough moment to make Julie's heart skip a beat. Mike was tall and trim, with dark eyes and black, wavy hair that always seemed perfectly maintained. His matinee-idol looks made him seem a likelier candidate to play a lawyer on TV than to be one in real life. Julie and Mike were friends in high school, during which she had occasional crushes on him. But she always felt he was a little out of her league.

"I'm sorry, you want to…" Mike gestured toward the dance floor.

Julie was slightly startled. She had not approached Mike at all expecting to dance but certainly had no reason to reject his invitation.

"Uh, sure," she managed, trying to sound more casual than the eagerness blaring inside her.

From across the gym floor, Julie glimpsed Van watching her slow dance with Mike for a moment, until he turned to throw away his punch cup and disappeared into the crowd.

"So, what have you been up to for the past, what, four years?" asked Mike.

"Actually, I've been up to the exact same thing since the last time we talked."

"Come on. I doubt that," said Mike. "Weren't you going to Australia or Japan or something?"

"I was. About a dozen times. But something always managed to keep me here." Julie hoped she did not sound too pathetic. She was not looking for sympathy. "Mainly saving up money because the itinerary just keeps growing."

"It's always something, right?"

"But, no excuses this time. My ticket is bought. Got a new giant backpack. New Year's Day, I'm leaving on a round-the-world trip. Who knows? I may not even come back."

"Well, that's kind of a bummer. Since I just got here."

They smiled at each other. Julie felt her face flush a bit, alarmed at the sudden flicker of infatuation she felt. She had so little genuine experience with anything resembling romance and was embarrassed that her mind was suddenly a chaotic press conference of blunt questions and deflections. She could not wait to depart on the trip she had been dreaming about for half her life, *but what if she stayed in Cedar Springs to marry Mike? But he has four children. She wasn't ready to be a mother. She couldn't give up New Zealand. Why was Mike smiling at her like this? Was he flirting? Did she represent the desperate Hail Mary of a lonely widower?* She fretted that perhaps accepting his invitation to dance had given him the wrong impression. She lamented her virtual lack of a dating life—no wonder these doubts and crazy thoughts were pulsing through her head. She had a recurring fear she might end up a spinster, and the incompetence she suddenly felt did not help the fear.

Cal Stevens returned to the microphone, snapping Julie from her pensive daze. She hoped she had not stared too awkwardly at Mike while she was shuffling through her thought-deck.

"Okay, everyone on the floor for the big swing dance-off!" directed Cal. "If you don't know how to swing, it doesn't matter. Just get out there and cut a rug!"

Julie and Mike looked at each other with expectant amusement.

"Do you remember it?" started Mike.

"Oh, man, I don't know," replied Julie with a grin. "Maybe."

Julie and Mike began the Swing dance routine they learned together in high school as dance partners for a senior choir class performance. They began slowly at first but were quickly amazed at their muscle memory. There were several missteps, but on the whole, the more they danced, the more they recalled the old routine.

"I can't believe how much of this I remember!" yelled Julie over the big-band music.

"Me neither!"

Julie and Mike continued the dance, laughing at themselves and having a blast. It grew quickly apparent to the other dancers and spectators that Julie and Mike were the best of a small handful of dancers who actually knew how to swing. Couples gradually dropped out and the crowd began to huddle around Julie and Mike, cheering them on.

As Julie continued dancing with aplomb, she saw Van's face at the back of the crowd. He smiled and clapped along, then gave Julie two thumbs up, though she couldn't tell if he was being encouraging or sarcastic. A moment later, she swung around and glimpsed Van again, curious as to why he now appeared to be quizzically looking up at the stage lights. Very soon, the reason for his investigation became quite clear.

Despite her vigorous movement, Julie tried to keep an eye on Van, following his suspicious gaze as best she could, which was fixated on the tall artificial Christmas tree on the left-hand side of the stage. Atop the tree was a prominent, student-made, paper angel from which a small plume of smoke now gently swirled upward. The paper angel brushed up against a very bright and undoubtedly hot stage light.

Suddenly, the paper angel burst into a small flame, which instantly spread around the top of the Christmas tree. Julie's eyes widened, then she abruptly stopped dancing and covered her mouth with her hands. Mike stopped dancing as well, looking confused until he noticed the object of Julie's shock. The loud music continued however, as most of the gym crowd remained blissfully ignorant of the flames. Julie watched Van dash a few steps over to the wall and grab a fire extinguisher. Before he could make it up the stage steps however, the top of the flaming tree crashed over against the painted bridge mural, which also quickly perished in flames. Yet Van continued onstage, attacking the tree and mural the best he could with the extinguisher.

It made Julie's heart glow to see her friend rush heroically toward the flames, but the fleeting feeling was doused by next-level chaos when the gymnasium's emergency sprinkler system engaged. Water instantly showered the entire floor, the booths, the food, the auction items, and the attendees. The music ground to a halt as the musicians tried in vain to protect their instruments. The crowd and dancers screamed, ran, slipped, and slid. Everyone was caught in the artificial downpour. Refreshments were trampled, the cider spilled. People slipped on food items and fell over each other in utter slapstick pandemonium.

Julie did her best to maintain her footing on the tarp-covered gym floor while she helped others to their feet who had been less successful. She got separated from Mike in the crowd as she assisted as many people as she could toward the exits. By the time the last person was safely outside, she was thoroughly soaked and befuddled by the evening's hairpin turn of events.

While Julie helped Van round up as many clean towels as they could find in the gym's locker rooms, Eric and his fellow firemen arrived to commandeer what remained of the hazard. Julie and Van hurried outside with the towels and distributed them to the shivering crowd. As they hastily handed out towels, Julie noticed Van skip over Mike's outstretched hand, and she wasn't entirely sure the oversight was accidental. That seemed rather odd of her pal, but she put a pin in the thought, and gave Mike a towel instead.

Moments later, Eric exited the gym in his full firefighter gear and approached Julie. "I heard you were burning up the dance floor. Does that mean all this is your fault?"

"*Ha, ha*," replied Julie sarcastically, her teeth still chattering.

"Good news is, the gym's going to make it. I hear Van's apparently the hero. Just a little damage to the stage. And they'll have to get a new Christmas tree," said Eric.

"Poor Mr. and Mrs. Mitchell," said Julie, "they put so much work into this."

A shivering Mike stepped closer to Julie with his towel wrapped tightly around his shoulders. "Can I give you a ride home?" he asked through chattering teeth.

Julie's mind sorted through several answers. She wanted to accept his invitation, but how would she explain having to return to the high school the next day to retrieve her own vehicle without having to admit her infatuation with Mike to her mom, dad, Aunt Bonnie, or Beth? She decided she would simply figure that one out later.

"Sure," she replied. "Thank you."

Eric overheard Mike's offer. Julie glanced at Eric who raised his eyebrows in silent, slightly amused reply.

Chapter 6

As Mike drove them away from the high school in his SUV, Julie felt ridiculous for accepting his invitation for such a short ride home. She did not mind the vehicle's luxurious interior, however, especially the warming feature of the leather seats, which was already working its magic on her frigid legs. She was not much of a student of car models, but noted the SUV was an Audi and it seemed expensive by her modest standards. She stole a glance in the back seat and noticed markers, bits of paper, a stuffed animal, and a fast-food cup—remnants leaving no mistake this was a family car. She also noticed Mike stayed diligently at or below the 30-mph speed limit but was not sure if he was just a law-abiding stickler or whether he was trying to prolong the very brief drive. Not that she necessarily opposed the latter because the seat-warmer felt majestic.

"Do you want to come over and meet my kids?" blurted Mike, just as they neared the turn to Julie's house off Main Street.

She was a bit taken aback. "In this condition?" she asked, glancing down at the towel still wrapped around her shoulders and kind of hoping it would be enough to dissuade him.

"My kids won't care. Would you mind? Just for a minute?"

Completely-dry-Julie would not have minded at all; wet hair, wet clothes, slightly-running-mascara-Julie, however, minded plenty. "Umm, well…okay…sure." *What had gotten into her?* First a non-essential ride home, now a potentially awkward interaction with children who would not necessarily approve of her presence.

"Great. The kids are going to love this."

"Why are they going to love it exactly?" she asked with amused suspicion.

"Because they've seen the video, many times, of high school dad swing-dancing with you in the choir concert thing."

"Oh, gosh. Is it too late to reconsider then?" she asked, only half-joking.

Mike made a couple quick lefts until they were heading north again, past the turn off for the high school.

Moments later, Julie was slightly startled when they pulled up to the Gilroy house, a long-vacant, formerly grand Victorian home that once belonged to one of the founders of Cedar Springs. No Gilroys had lived in Cedar Springs for decades and the house had fallen into disrepair. Everyone in town could see the house had potential, yet, until now, no buyer was willing to confront the vast remodeling labor and expense required to make it livable again.

"You're kidding," said Julie, "you're living in the old Gilroy house?"

"Yep. Bought it just a few weeks ago."

"Wow. You're way braver than I am."

"Karen and I always thought it was a diamond in the rough. She used to dream of turning it into a B&B."

Julie and her parents often mentioned the same idea in passing over the years, but running Shelly's kept them more than busy enough to ever seriously contemplate such an undertaking.

"So, Mom's going to help me do it."

"You're actually turning this into a Bed & Breakfast?"

"Yep. Pretty cool huh? I mean, the B&B part's still several years away, but…"

Julie looked out the window and raised her eyebrows. She did not mean to appear skeptical, but she had never actually examined the house this closely before and even in the dark she could tell the reclamation task looked formidable. Mike sensed her skepticism.

"It looks a lot better on the inside," he said.

Julie was not so sure, but they exited the car and she followed him inside the house. The door creaked loudly as he opened and closed it behind them.

"Hello?" called Mike.

Four rowdy children materialized in a flash with shouts of "Daddy!" Mike's mother, Sarah, wearily descended the stairs well behind the children.

"I didn't expect you back so early," said Sarah in a rather sullen tone.

"Yeah, the event was kind of a wash-out," replied Mike as he scooped up his youngest daughter.

"Eww, Daddy, you're wet!" said the girl.

"I know! I didn't know I was going to need my swimsuit tonight." Mike swiveled around, acknowledging Julie. "Okay, so everyone, this is Julie."

Julie waved a bit sheepishly. She was still uneasy about her decision to drop by like this, unannounced.

"Julie, you remember my mom, Sarah," continued Mike.

"Yes, hi!" said Julie, trying to strike the right friendly tone without sounding like she was presenting herself as Sarah's imminent daughter-in-law.

"Hello," replied Sarah in a reserved manner that already made Julie a bit anxious.

Mike continued his introductions, unbothered by his mother's unsmiling demeanor, nodding in the direction of each of his four children, starting with the daughter in his arms. "And this is Zuzu...Pete...that's Janie...and Tommy."

"Very nice to meet you all," said Julie, smiling.

"And yes, in case you were wondering, we did name them after George Bailey's kids from *It's a Wonderful Life*," said Mike.

Other than Zuzu, Julie did not remember those were the Bailey kids' names in the movie. Now that he pointed it out however, she found it rather odd.

"It was Karen's favorite movie," Mike explained matter-of-factly.

"I see," managed Julie, not sure how else to react. "It's funny because I'd never seen that movie before, until the other day..."

Julie's cell phone rang at full volume, piercing the air and cutting short her thought. Her ringtone was B.J. Thomas singing, "As Long as We've Got Each Other," the theme song from the 1980s TV series *Growing Pains*. It was a jokey ringtone selection made with Beth one late night several years ago. They selected it in tribute to the sitcom they liked to watch in reruns together when they were in junior high. She was startled and somewhat embarrassed by the song in her current circumstance. Mike's smile, however, seemed to indicate he found her choice of ringtone amusing.

She quickly dug the phone out of her small purse, glanced at the screen and said, "Sorry, excuse me," as she answered it. "Hey, Mom." She listened intently as her mom's quivering voice delivered news that her dad had suffered a heart attack and was on his way to the hospital by ambulance. Julie assured her mom she would meet her at the hospital right away.

Julie lowered the phone and looked at Mike with panic in her eyes. "My dad had a heart attack. I've got to go."

"I'll drive," said Mike, quickly lowering Zuzu to the floor and following Julie swiftly out the front door.

Chapter 7

Mike flew them across town in his SUV, destroying his earlier prudence in obeying the speed limits. He ripped through the parking lot, halting directly in front of the automatic double doors of the emergency room entrance. He offered to accompany Julie, but she insisted it was unnecessary and thanked him for the ride. She jogged inside and quickly found her mom and Bonnie in the E.R. waiting room.

The three of them joined hands and prayed silently for a few minutes as they sat. Then, an excruciating half-hour wait ensued, until a doctor wearing surgical scrubs mercifully arrived to inform them Perry was stable. The doctor confirmed it had indeed been a heart attack, but Perry was now out of the woods.

After another half-hour wait, Julie and Bev were finally admitted to Perry's quiet, lamp-lit room, where they found him sleeping. Julie teared up at the sight of her robust, energetic father suddenly helpless and ashen, his strong, industrious arms lifeless at his side, tethered to wires and tubes. She caught her breath and restrained her tears the best she could, wanting to be brave for her mom's sake.

After sitting quietly for a while at Perry's bedside, Bev broke the anxious tension by inquiring about Julie's evening at the benefit. Julie apprised her mom of the strange sequence of events, the dancing with Mike, the peculiar gymnasium fire, and briefly meeting Mike's family. An hour later, with Perry still asleep and Bev semi-dozing in a chair beside him, Julie decided to stretch her legs and check on Bonnie in the waiting room.

In the meager hospital cafeteria, Julie bought two cups of coffee from a vending machine that looked like it was a remnant of the facility's original early-1980s construction. On the way back to the waiting room, she rounded a corner into a hallway where a nurse was pushing Harriet Paddock in a wheelchair. Julie considered a sudden pivot to avoid crossing paths with Harriet, but it was too late to change course without drawing more attention to herself. Reluctantly, she steeled her nerves and continued walking toward Harriet and the nurse. Julie quickly discerned an argument in progress.

"Wouldn't you much rather get a decent night's sleep in your own home, Ms. Paddock?" asked the nurse hopefully.

"I told that other nurse already..." said Harriet.

"*Sylvia*," interjected the nurse, indicating "that other nurse" had a name.

"I'm not going anywhere until my condition fully stabilizes! Now it is your *job* to see that it does."

"Which it already *has*," replied the nurse.

"You know Doctor what's-his-name doesn't know what he's talking about. Ink's still drying on his medical diploma, if he has one. Is Dr. Merritt on duty? I demand a second opinion!"

"Now, Ms. Paddock, you're getting all worked up again."

"I told you, I'm not leaving until my condition—"

"Stabilizes," said the nurse, cutting her off, "we know."

Harriet glanced up in time to see Julie approaching, which made Julie feel like she must at least greet Harriet. "Hello, Ms. Paddock. Everything okay?" asked Julie, with as much sincerity as she could muster toward Harriet.

The nurse stopped pushing the wheelchair as they reached Julie.

"Most certainly not! All that smoke from the high school fire aggravated my asthmatic condition. Nearly killed me," growled Harriet.

Behind Harriet's back, the nurse squinted and shook her head at Julie, indicating death had not been a risk for Harriet that evening.

"Sorry to hear that. I didn't realize the smoke blew that far across town," replied Julie with a dash of sarcasm.

Harriet glared at Julie. "My asthma's already worse than it's ever been. Gets worse every year thanks to the traffic smog from your little Christmas light show," continued Harriet.

"Yes, I've heard you're not a fan of the lights," said Julie exhaustedly. She was in no mood for a Harriet confrontation. She only greeted Harriet because they could not avoid passing in the hallway, and because she still occasionally thought that somewhere beneath Harriet's thick layers of bitterness must surely beat a human heart with actual feelings. That thought grew fainter, however, with each new encounter with Harriet.

"What are you doing here? Your aunt misplace her brain again?" asked Harriet with a snarly grin.

"Dad had a heart attack," replied Julie matter-of-factly.

Harriet's smirk faded. "Oh. Well. Sorry."

"Thank the Lord, the ambulance got there in time," said Julie.

"Indeed," muttered Harriet. "Hope he's okay."

Julie considered letting Harriet know how yet another lawsuit undoubtedly contributed to Perry's heart attack but restrained herself. "Thanks," said Julie, continuing down the hallway. Behind her, Harriet's animated health debate with the nurse resumed.

Julie reached the waiting room and sat beside Aunt Bonnie, handing her one of the cups of coffee. A pre-teen boy sat nearby, channel-surfing the large television, which hung on the wall at the opposite end of the room. Bonnie took a sip of her coffee and put an appreciative arm around Julie.

They sat in silence for a moment, except for the diverse sounds of the revolving TV channels. Julie glanced to her right and noticed a book sitting atop a pile of old magazines on the lamp table. The book's cover was quite worn and slightly ripped, but the title was still readable: *The Adventures of Huckleberry Finn*. Curious, Julie picked up the book and opened its cover. On the first page was a handwritten inscription in black ink, which she read to herself.

"Check this out," said Julie quietly to Bonnie.

Julie handed the opened book to Bonnie, who read the inscription aloud: "*Dear Reader, Remember no man is a failure who has friends. Love, Doctor Swerling.*"

Julie grinned expectantly. "You know what that's from?"

"Doctor Swerling?" replied Bonnie with a grin.

"That was in *It's a Wonderful Life*. At the end, remember? That's what the angel writes to George in the book he gives him."

Bonnie handed the book back to Julie. "I haven't seen that movie in ages."

A middle-aged woman appeared in the waiting room entryway. "Hunter, come on, let's go," she said.

The channel-surfing boy tossed the remote control in the chair beside him and followed the woman out of the waiting room. The channel he left on the TV was airing *It's a Wonderful Life*. Julie stared at the screen, intrigued. She set her coffee cup on the lamp table beside her and stepped over to pick up the abandoned remote control. She sat back down and turned up the volume just in time to hear George Bailey's uncle, Billy, suddenly interrupt George and Mary's flirtatious stroll with the news that George's father had a stroke.

Julie subtly shook her head, dumbfounded, recalling the events of the past several hours. She glanced at Bonnie, who had her head leaned back against the wall, resting with her eyes closed.

Bev suddenly entered the waiting room and Julie stood to meet her. "He's awake now. He's talking. He's very weak, but he's asking for you," said Bev.

Julie hugged her mother tightly, then followed Bev back to her father's bedside.

Chapter 8

The next day, Julie and Aunt Bonnie kept the SB&C running while Bev stayed at the hospital with Perry. Shortly after noon, Julie called her mom for an update. She was relieved to hear that her dad rested well through the morning, ate part of a meal, and that her mom thought his normal color was returning to his face. Bev explained that though Perry's vital signs trended upward, his doctor advised him to remain at the hospital a couple nights as a precaution. Julie knew her dad would mildly resist staying the extra nights but ultimately relent, since Bev concurred with the doctor. Perry trusted his wife implicitly.

The afternoon was rather low-key at the café, allowing Julie to catch up on inventory behind the counter. She welcomed the interruption of Beth and Eric, however, who stopped in for a short break, as was their custom several times a week. Julie poured them free cups of coffee and Bonnie sliced Eric an unsolicited piece of pumpkin pie, which he eagerly accepted. Beth and Eric sat on the stools at the counter, conversing with Julie while she tidied up. Julie was preoccupied with her father and his condition but thinking about him in the hospital reminded her of the waiting room and the curious book inscription.

"Ever since I watched *It's a Wonderful Life* with y'all, it's been popping up everywhere," said Julie.

"It's just one of those movies, you know, it's part of the culture," offered Eric in a rare, semi-contemplative observation.

"But I mean it's been *everywhere*, every time I turn around. In odd ways," continued Julie.

"Maybe you're just noticing it now because you hadn't seen it before," said Beth as she helped herself to a bite of Eric's pumpkin pie.

"I guess. Maybe. But there seems to be more to it than that. I don't know, it's almost like…" Julie paused from wiping the counter.

"What?" asked Beth curiously.

"Nothing. It sounds ridiculous," said Julie.

"I love ridiculous-sounding stuff. Bring it on," said Eric, with a mouthful of pie.

Beth leaned forward confidentially. "Go ahead. It's just us."

Julie paused again with a sigh. "Okay. Well…if I wasn't totally sane, which I am, I'd think my life was somehow, like, mirroring parts of the movie. Or something."

Eric cracked up. Beth smiled, but tried to appear open-minded for her friend's sake.

Julie waved her hand dismissively at Eric's laughter. "I know. See? I'm already sorry I said it."

"This is awesome!" Eric said.

"Ignore him," said Beth, "What do you mean?"

"I'm not really sure, except there are all these parallels."

"Like?" asked Beth.

"Okay, last night alone, there was the dance where I ran into Mike Hughes whom I haven't seen in years. We had like this instant spark and we were dancing in the swing contest, and then the fire sprinklers went off and we got soaked. Sound familiar?"

Beth thought for a moment. "Okay, so like George and Mary falling into the pool under the dance floor?"

"Precisely!" said Julie.

"What else?" urged Beth.

"So, it turns out Mike's renovating that old Gilroy house, just like Mary does in the movie. Plus, did you know his four kids are named after the kids in the movie?"

"Who would do that? That's kinda weird," chimed Eric, incredulous and now fully amused.

Beth continued ignoring him and said, "Okay, I just got chills."

"That proves it then!" mocked Eric. "She's got chills. It's officially magic." He rolled his eyes at Beth and Julie, made a slight scoffing noise, and took another bite of his pie.

"I haven't even got to the kicker yet," said Julie, addressing Eric's none-too-subtle skepticism.

"Your dad's heart attack!" blurted Beth as if solving a mystery. She covered her mouth with both hands.

Julie shrugged in an *I told you so* fashion.

"Okay, I admit, that's some quality coincidence," relented Eric.

"So, you're like a female George Bailey!" exclaimed Beth.

"Apparently so," replied Julie with a grin.

"The question is, *why*?" asked Eric, relishing his own sarcasm.

Aunt Bonnie entered from the kitchen, oblivious to the conversation, with flour on her apron and a pen tucked behind her ear. "I keep forgetting, Julie, when are you leaving on your big trip? We need to check with Teresa to make sure she can still work full time while you're gone."

Teresa was Julie's twenty-five-year-old cousin, the only daughter of Bev's older sister. Teresa lived near her parents in

Nags Head, North Carolina. Over the years, she often worked at Shelly's during summer breaks and holidays.

"January first," replied Julie. She was certain she had informed Bonnie a dozen times about her departure date, but she made it a baker's dozen reminders. She knew it would likely take several more. She also knew her mother already confirmed plans with Teresa, who would arrive next week and board in Julie's old room in her parents' house. Then, after Julie's departure on her trip, Teresa would move into Julie's flat above the garage where she would live while working at Shelly's for the remainder of Julie's year abroad. Bev and Julie had already been over the details with Bonnie, but would apparently have to do so again.

Beth leaned over the counter toward Julie and whispered out of Bonnie's earshot, "She's kind of like George's uncle in the movie!"

"Oh my gosh, I didn't even think of that one!"

"Ladies," interjected Eric, "if you start looking hard enough, I'm sure you can find parallels in tons of movies. I mean, I went jogging this morning and lifted some weights. It doesn't mean I'm turning into Rocky. *Yo*," he said, in a poor attempt at his best Rocky Balboa voice, "that'd be pretty *sweet*, though."

At that moment, Julie's brother, Hugh, quietly slipped in the café entrance wearing his U.S. Coast Guard uniform. Holding his hand was a petite blonde woman sharply dressed in jeans, a sweater, and boots.

Hugh stood still just inside the entrance and cleared his throat. "Is the pie any good here?"

Wide-eyed, Julie spun toward Hugh and let out an excited squeal. She rushed out from behind the counter with Bonnie close behind.

"I didn't think you'd be able to make it!" said Julie, embracing her brother.

"I got here as soon as I could," replied Hugh. Bonnie stepped in for her hug. "Aunt Bonnie! You look exactly the same. Not a day over eighty-five!"

Bonnie slapped his arm. "You turkey! How 'bout this uniform though?" asked Bonnie, looking at Julie, "Does your brother look like a recruitment poster, or what?"

Hugh was three years older than Julie and, at least in her eyes, significantly wiser and more accomplished than her. She had always looked up to him in both the admirable and literal sense (he was nearly a foot taller than her). He always took his protective older brother role seriously, with a generous side of teasing, joking, and general pestering for good measure. Hugh was a helicopter pilot in the United States Coast Guard, stationed in Jacksonville, Florida. His demanding schedule left little time to visit home more than a few times a year. Though he had lived out of state for several years, Julie still missed her brother's camaraderie. He was good about calling her on the phone at least once a week and prioritized her out-of-the-blue calls and randomly texted gifs as much as his rigorous Coast Guard duties allowed. She was proud of her big brother's military service and pilot skills, but she looked forward to a time when he might be able to move somewhere closer to Cedar Springs. With their dad in the hospital, she felt tremendous relief to have Hugh home.

"Have you been to see Dad yet?" asked Julie.

"Yeah, we just came from the hospital," replied Hugh. "He's doing pretty well considering. He was really surprised to see us."

Julie glanced at the woman holding her brother's hand, who beamed a slightly shy smile. Julie had never met her before and was suddenly quite curious. As if Hugh read her mind he said, "And, speaking of surprises…I have another kind of big one. I'd like you to meet Robyn McFarland…the future Mrs. Shelly!"

Julie's jaw dropped.

"Come again?" asked Aunt Bonnie.

"We're getting married!" clarified Hugh.

"You dork!" blurted Julie. "We didn't even know you were dating someone. Congratulations!"

Julie and Bonnie gushed and exchanged more hugs with Hugh and Robyn, who eagerly held up her engagement ring for their admiring inspection.

Beth and Eric drifted from the counter to join Julie. In the commotion, Beth subtly leaned close to Julie's ear and said, "Just like Harry Bailey when he shows up with his new bride!"

Julie and Beth exchanged astonished looks. Julie stumbled backward a couple steps and momentarily steadied herself on a table before slumping to a chair. She felt like she was going to faint. She had never officially fainted before, but she was almost certain this was what it felt like. Hugh, Eric, and Beth scrambled to help steady her.

"Whoa, you okay?" asked Hugh.

Julie's eyes fluttered a bit. She felt slightly disoriented and saw a smattering of sparks in her vision. Beth hurried behind the counter and returned with a cold, wet towel, which she held to Julie's forehead.

"Deep breaths," offered Beth.

"I'm okay. I just feel a little light-headed all the sudden," said Julie slowly. "I'm probably just tired. I haven't had much sleep the past couple days." Julie put her hand to the towel on her head and tried to stand.

"Easy…" said Hugh, holding her arm for support.

Julie closed her eyes and inhaled slowly a few times before she opened her right eye, peeked up at Hugh and asked, "You're seriously engaged?"

"Yep," replied Hugh with a wide grin.

Julie looked at Robyn who stood in the concerned huddle surrounding Julie. "And let me guess—your dad probably owns some kind of business and he offered Hugh a job when he gets out of the Coast Guard."

"Actually, my *grandfather* owns his own business, so, who knows? Maybe someday. How did you know?" wondered Robyn, looking rather confused.

"Lucky guess," replied Julie, sharing a knowing look with Beth.

"Well, nothing's set in stone yet," said Hugh. "Except that we're getting married."

Julie grinned at Hugh, gingerly shaking her head. "This is so weird."

Chapter 9

The following morning, Bev was back at work at Shelly's, with Hugh and Robyn keeping Perry company at the hospital. Just after ten o'clock, as the busiest shift of the day wound down, Julie removed her apron and hung it on the hook beside the swinging door in the kitchen. She announced she was going to the library, leaving Bev and Aunt Bonnie to helm the café for a spell. Julie exited the café's front door, turned left on the sidewalk, and walked briskly down Main Street on a mission.

As she came to the end of the block and was about to cross the street, a pickup truck approached from Julie's left, almost splashing her with cold slush from the road's icy puddles as it approached the stop sign. Julie leapt back to avoid the splash and glanced up at the guilty party when the truck rolled to a stop. The truck's passenger side window lowered to reveal Harriet behind the steering wheel.

"You know, there *is* a way to avoid all this courtroom rig-marole," said Harriet, practically yelling out the window to be heard over her truck's engine.

"Oh, really? How's that exactly?" asked Julie.

"Simple. Just talk your hard-headed father into turning off the lights."

"Just like that, huh? No more lawsuits? No more dousing Christmas cheer?"

"Christmas cheer isn't the problem. This thing has been a total pain in the public's backside for years. I'm doing this town a favor!"

"Is that what you tell yourself to sleep at night?"

"All you have to do is pull the plug and I'll drop the lawsuit."

"Okay, well I'll be sure *not* to pass that on to Dad, who's still in the hospital by the way. Thanks for asking. Glad to see *you* made such a miraculous recovery."

Julie surprised herself at the forceful manner in which she sometimes spoke to Harriet. She never talked to anyone else that way. She was not proud of it per se, though in this case it felt good to stand up for her family.

Harriet grimaced and gripped the steering wheel tightly. "You know what your family's problem is?"

"Do tell."

"Your ridiculous pride. Those gaudy lights are just an ego thing for the Shellys. Always have been. And it's not about spreading Christmas cheer. It's about Christmas commerce and peddling those overrated cookies!"

"Merry Christmas, Harriet!" Julie gave Harriet a brief, dismissive wave then crossed the street in front of the truck. She glided down the sidewalk, trying to sweep Harriet from her mind. Fuming, Harriet rolled down her driver's side window to share a parting barb with Julie. But she failed to concoct the right phrase in a timely fashion, so she rolled up the window, smashed her foot on the gas pedal and sped away.

Julie's mid-morning destination was one of her lifelong favorite spots in town: the Cedar Springs Public Library. She pushed through the library's weighty, original 1930s art-deco doors and slowly inhaled. She always enjoyed the distinct scent of aged paper and creaky book bindings—the smell of history. Every time that scent washed over her, she was five years old again, following Bev to the circulation desk, struggling under the heft of picture books stacked high on her wobbly, featherweight arms.

She sat at a computer station and began her Internet trawl by typing, "*It's a Wonderful Life history*" in the search box. She could have saved the research for her laptop computer at home, but she could not rid her mind of the coincidences of the past several days and wanted to satisfy her curiosity right away. Her smartphone was little help in that regard as it was an older, clunky model and she disliked trying to read anything in-depth on its relatively tiny screen. Besides, she loved the library and its exclusive archival resources, plus, its lightning-fast Internet connection was preferable to the often-spotty Wi-Fi connection in her garage apartment.

Julie's online research revealed tidbits she found intriguing, as she had zero previous knowledge of *It's a Wonderful Life* lore. She was surprised to learn the film's script was based on a short story called *The Greatest Gift* by an author and historian named Philip Van Doren Stern. She read how in 1943, Stern printed two hundred copies of his short story in booklet form and mailed it as a Christmas card to relatives and friends. One of those booklets eventually found its way to a producer at RKO Pictures, which bought the movie rights to Stern's short story, then sold them to director Frank Capra in 1945. Under Capra's guidance, *The Greatest Gift* became the film *It's a Wonderful Life*, released in late 1946. Julie was further surprised to discover such a revered movie had actually been an overall failure at the box office, despite being critically acclaimed and receiving five Academy Award nominations, including Best Picture.

For every nugget Julie unearthed however, she found infinitely more flimflam. She wondered what percentage of the Internet is actually comprised of annoying lists—*five surprising facts about…ten things you didn't know about…twenty-five reasons you should check out…*

Julie glanced at her watch, surprised an hour had evaporated so quickly. She grew weary of wading through the minefield of blogs and click bait. She now knew more about the movie and its making but was disappointed she had not discovered anything that might remotely shed light on her recent peculiar circumstances. She had no clue what to look for; she was simply hoping to strike gold immediately out of the gate.

She pulled her phone from her pocket and sent a text to her mom inquiring about the status of the café. Bev replied promptly, assuring Julie all was well and to take her time. Bev was accustomed to Julie's library excursions so she didn't probe as to the nature of this particular trip.

Julie abandoned the computer terminal for her favorite vintage library technology—the microfiche machine in the very back of the single-story building. Perusing the microfiche files with the machine's clunky knobs and antiquated screen was a nerdy, analog pleasure for her. It always made her feel like an old-fashioned journalist on a sleuthing quest. She loved digging into decades-old issues of newspapers. Not that it was a regular recreational activity for her, but on rare occasions reaching back to her teenage years, she happily whiled away hours at a time inspecting old newspapers, researching topics of interest or poring over articles by her favorite writers.

Having learned *It's a Wonderful Life* debuted in theatres in December 1946, Julie located the microfiche containing issues of the *Cedar Springs Sentinel* from 1946 and 1947. The *Sentinel* had always been a weekly paper, so it did not take her long to browse multiple issues. After another half hour vanished with no interesting discoveries, she was about to abandon her inquiry when her eyes widened at a small headline that she almost scrolled past. At the top of the back page of the March 11, 1947 issue, the headline read: *Cedar Springs Resident Meets Hollywood Stars Jimmy Stewart and Frank Capra.*

Julie's eyes bored through the brief article, her pulse quickening as she ingested the information. The Cedar Springs "resident" from the article's headline was none other than Julie's paternal grandmother, Hope Shelly. As the article explained, Hope traveled to Beaumont, Texas, in late February 1947 to visit her cousin Ruth, who had given birth to her first child, a girl, one month earlier. In the middle of the second week of her two-week visit, Hope, Ruth, and other extended family members were among scores of residents who flocked downtown Beaumont to glimpse Jimmy Stewart and Frank Capra riding in an open-topped car down Main Street in a parade in their honor. Stewart and Capra were apparently in Beaumont for a specially arranged promotional stop for their new movie, *It's a Wonderful Life*. After the parade, the Beaumont mayor presented Stewart and Capra with keys to the city in a ceremony outside City Hall. It was there, according to the *Sentinel* article, that Stewart and Capra posed for photos with many townsfolk, including Hope Shelly and her cousin.

Julie scrolled frantically to the next page, desperately hoping to find the photo. But it was not there.

She glanced around the nearly empty library, completely dumbfounded. She could not fathom what, if anything, this random connection between the movie and her late grandmother could possibly have to do with Julie and her own unusual recent circumstances. But she was fascinated. What were the odds that her grandmother would be in Beaumont, Texas, of all places, and that these particular Hollywood personalities would have visited that particular small town at the same time?

Julie searched her jeans pockets for change in vain. She hurried to the help desk near the library entrance and asked an elderly lady named Nancy (Julie was on a first-name basis with all the librarians) if she could borrow a dime to make a copy. Nancy gladly spotted her the necessary coinage, which Julie fed into the ancient copier attached to the microfiche machine, printing out the article about Hope Shelly's 1947 visit to Beaumont, Texas.

Julie nabbed her photocopy of the article, thanked Nancy again, and rushed out of the library, jogging most of the way back to the SB&C. As soon as she arrived, she hoped to glean more information from her mom, but Bev had already left to visit Perry in the hospital. Instead, Julie hustled back behind the counter where Bonnie was stowing freshly cleaned coffee mugs.

"Where's the fire?" asked Bonnie, referencing Julie's frenzied state.

"Do you remember your mother ever talking about getting to meet Jimmy Stewart and Frank Capra in Beaumont, Texas?" Julie did not hold out much hope that her relative with the worst recall in the family would be up to the challenge of such a question, but Bonnie was her only currently available source.

Bonnie paused her coffee mug task to ponder for a moment. "No. Don't remember anything like that." Bonnie tapped herself on the temple with her forefinger. "But, the ol' computer ain't quite what it used to be. Seems like Mother did have a cousin who lived in Texas at one time."

"According to the paper she did." Julie eagerly unfolded her library article and handed it to Bonnie.

Bonnie perused the article long enough to make Julie wonder if she should tackle another chore around the café while awaiting her aunt's response.

"Well, I'll be," Bonnie finally offered, "Yes. Seems like I do remember something about that once upon a time."

Julie looked at Bonnie, expecting something else to follow her aunt's remark. But there was nothing more. New customers entered the café, so Julie accepted the article back from Bonnie, folded it up, and returned it to her back jeans pocket. Her investigation would have to wait.

※ ※ ※

The following evening, after closing time at the SB&C, Julie accompanied her mom, Hugh, and Robyn back to the hospital where Perry was being released to go home. Julie savored the smiles of relief that enveloped her dad's face once he was finally settled into his favorite living room recliner. Julie spread a blanket across his lap and placed the TV remote on the armrest of his chair. Perry expressed appreciation for their help and concern, insisting there was no need for so much fuss over him. He told Julie that he did not feel as fragile as everyone was treating him but felt blessed to have such an attentive, loving family.

Soon, Perry fell asleep watching television and the family moved their conversation to the dining room so as not to disturb his nap. Before Julie retired to her flat for the night, she remembered to ask her mother if she recalled where they stashed the boxes of old photographs and mementos they found when remodeling the SB&C several years ago. Bev was not exactly sure, but suggested Julie try their attic.

✳ ✳ ✳

Two days later, on a cold, rainy Sunday afternoon, Julie sequestered herself in her parents' attic, determined to conduct an exhaustive search for the 1947 photograph of her grandmother. She had been sifting through boxes for almost an hour when Beth arrived to chat and check on Julie's progress. In short order, Beth was on the attic floor beside Julie, equally ensconced in the quest.

After another hour of diligent digging and even more diligent laughter, Beth was two-thirds of the way through her fourth tattered box of photos when she hit the jackpot. She pulled out a 4x6 black & white photograph with a white border that was a bit worn at the edges. In the photo, Hope Shelly and her cousin, Ruth, stood between Jimmy Stewart and Frank Capra in downtown Beaumont, Texas. Beth nonchalantly held up the photo for Julie's inspection, waiting silently until Julie finally glanced up from the box in her own lap. Julie gasped and took the photo carefully from Beth. She stood up from the floor, holding it closer to the overhead light bulb for inspection.

"I don't believe it," said Julie.

"Who's the other dude?" inquired Beth

"Frank Capra," replied Julie matter-of-factly.

"Who's Frank Capra?"

"How many times have you seen that movie? He was the director. I'm the one who'd never seen it before, and *I* know who Frank Capra is."

"Yeah, well, you're a nerd like that, okay? I never pay attention to the credits." Beth pointed to Hope Shelly in the photo. "And that's your grandmother?"

"Apparently so," said Julie shaking her head. "I haven't seen many photos of her when she was that young. She's so pretty."

"I don't know why, but I'm kind of freaked out," said Beth.

"I know!"

"But what does all this have to do with you?" wondered Beth.

"Absolutely no clue," replied Julie. "But it's got to be something, right?"

Beth shrugged her shoulders and held them there. "I mean, it's pretty cool, but I guess coincidence *is* the likeliest explanation. Maybe you should watch the movie again for clues or something."

Julie let it all sink in for a brief, silent moment, then vigorously shook her head. "This is nuts. I'm nuts! I've stayed way too long in my safe little insulated small-town world and now I'm finally cracking!"

Beth clasped her hand on Julie's shoulder in playful reassurance. "You're not nuts. Your life just happens to be somehow weirdly connected with one of the most cherished movie classics of all time. That's all."

Julie gave her an exasperated *you're-not-helping* look.

The attic door creaked open and Bev entered. Julie triumphantly held aloft the photograph.

"Oh, did you find it?" asked Bev.

"Beth did," replied Julie.

Bev studied the photo in the light and shook her head. "Amazing. Look at Hope—such a beautiful young woman!"

"Mom, I was thinking we should throw a surprise engagement party for Hugh and Robyn before they have to leave."

"I think that's a great idea," replied Bev, handing the photo back to Julie.

"You think Dad will be up for that?"

"Yeah, I think so. When were you thinking?"

"Well, aren't they leaving Tuesday?"

"That sounds right."

"So we'd have to do it tomorrow night. I could volunteer Beth to help us out." Julie grinned at Beth. "We should be able to throw something together."

"For sure!" said Beth. "Eric *loves* being dragged to last-minute social gatherings. It's his favorite."

Chapter 10

Barely twenty-four hours after Julie suggested the idea, the Shellys' house bustled with an engagement party for Hugh and Robyn. The living and dining rooms were warm and festive, fully adorned with Christmas tree and decorations. In keeping with their longstanding tradition, Julie had helped her mother put up the tree on the first Sunday afternoon following Thanksgiving. Once Julie and Bev hashed out the particulars of the engagement party, Julie sent a mass email invitation and crossed her fingers people would show up on such short notice. Her worry was unfounded however because the house was ultimately filled with friends and extended family.

Perry still appeared weak to those familiar with his usual vigorous capacity, but he felt strong enough to get dressed up for the occasion in a collared shirt, sweater, and khaki pants. Perry was old-fashioned that way. If there were guests coming over, no matter whom it was, he would look respectable. He sat in his favorite recliner close to the fireplace. Hugh and Robyn beamed from their perch on the brick ledge in front of the fire as well wishers milled about, eating, drinking, and congratulating the couple.

Julie meandered through the living room serving hot cider to the guests. Beth followed close behind her with a tray of frosted sugar cookies. After making a couple leisurely rounds through the living and dining rooms, Julie and Beth set down their trays in the kitchen.

"So, have you figured out what's going to happen to you next?" joked Beth in a hushed, secretive tone.

Julie had tried all day, mostly unsuccessfully, *not* to dwell on the *Wonderful Life* mystery and now Beth was dredging it up again. "No," scoffed Julie. "But…" She caught herself, suddenly feeling too foolish to admit anything further, even to her best friend.

"What?"

"I don't know," said Julie, holding tight to the reins of what she was afraid to share.

"Yes, you do. Out with it!"

"You know I don't do tingly, touchy-feely, finding-meaning-behind-every-dream kind of stuff."

"Right. Right," Beth prodded eagerly.

"And you know how it annoys me when people go around saying that God *told* them such and such. Because I think people throw that around too loosely."

"Yes, I know this about you."

"Not that God doesn't speak to people, I just think it's rarer than a lot of people think."

"You think God's trying to tell you something?" asked Beth, with growing impatience.

"Maybe? Or like, maybe something big's going to happen? Maybe some kind of…I don't know what exactly." Julie gauged Beth's reaction and decided to take the edge off the potential craziness of her statements. "Maybe find out my life's purpose? How awesome would that be?"

"Wait, you're not secretly depressed, are you?" asked Beth as the notion struck her for the first time. "Because George Bailey definitely gets depressed. If people had just recognized the warning signs, he could've seen a shrink and saved ol' Clarence the trip."

"I'm not depressed," insisted Julie. "I mean, I'm not necessarily overjoyed all the time, but who is?"

"Not me," agreed Beth. "But what if you *are* depressed, and you just don't realize it?"

"You're kind of depressing me now."

"Maybe you should spend some time soul-searching. Get into nature or something. Maybe go for a hike."

"Get into nature?" Julie loved her friend's sense of humor.

"Yeah. When's the last time you had any quality alone time?"

"I don't know. Never? Why do you think I've been trying to go travel the world by myself?"

Julie and Beth cracked up laughing.

✳ ✳ ✳

Just after ten o'clock, as the party slowly dwindled, Julie drove Aunt Bonnie home. Bonnie lived less than two miles from the Shellys' house, but she no longer liked to drive herself any distance after dark.

"What a night!" said Bonnie excitedly as she rode in the front passenger seat. "Can you believe your brother getting engaged like that without telling us? What a rascal! And Perry already home from the hospital! It's shaping up to be quite a Christmas. Now if we just go toilet paper Harriet's house or something, we can complete the trifecta!"

"That *is* tempting," said Julie, grinning at Bonnie. Julie enjoyed her aunt's mischievous side.

Julie made a right turn into the short driveway in front of Bonnie's small brick house. When Julie was in elementary school, Bonnie and her late husband, Tom, lived in a farmhouse on thirty acres outside Cedar Springs. After Tom died of cancer fifteen years ago, however, Bonnie sold their house and land. She then moved into the two-bedroom house in town to be closer to the café, but mainly to be closer to Perry, Bev, and Julie. They were Bonnie's only immediate family as she and Tom were unable to have children.

Bonnie got out of the car rather slowly, then realized she was missing something. "Fiddlesticks," she said, "I don't have my keys."

Julie reached into her own coat pocket, pulled out Bonnie's keys, and reached across the passenger seat to hand them to her.

"Oh! Thank you!" said Bonnie.

Julie pulled Bonnie's phone from her other coat pocket and handed it to Bonnie as well.

"And here's your phone."

"Oh my gosh! Totally forgot."

"No worries."

"Don't know what I'd do without you, dear. Seriously." Bonnie blew her a kiss. "Good night."

"Good night."

Bonnie made her way to the front door of her house, humming "It's Beginning to Look a Lot Like Christmas" as she went. She forgot to close the passenger side door, so Julie leaned across the seat to pull it closed. Julie patiently waited until Bonnie unlocked the front door of her house and made it safely inside before backing out of the driveway and returning home.

When Julie arrived, she found Bev hauling two trash bags out the side door of the house. Julie quickly exited her car to help.

"I'll take care of that, Mom."

"It's okay. I've got it."

Julie took the bags from Bev anyway, put them in the trashcan, and secured the lid.

"So, what do you think of your surprise future sister-in-law?" asked Bev.

Julie glimpsed Hugh and Robyn through the kitchen window, laughing and talking with a few lingering friends.

"I think Hugh hit the jackpot. She seems fantastic," replied Julie, smiling.

"Yeah, I think she'll be able to keep him in line."

"I doubt they'll end up back in Cedar Springs when he gets out of the Coast Guard though," said Julie with a tinge of sadness in her voice.

"Are you worried about it affecting your travel plans?"

"Maybe a little. With Dad's heart and everything, it's not the best time for me to be leaving. But then, I kind of feel like if I don't stick with my plan, I'll be stuck here forever." Julie glanced at her mom, wishing she could retract saying *stuck*. "I'm sorry. That's a bad way to put it."

"I know what you mean. You've always been here for us even when it wasn't necessarily what you wanted. You have a gift for making the best of situations. Just one of the many things I love about you. Actually, it's the first thing I remember about you as a baby. You had the most glowing smile. Lord knows what all you'd been through, but it was almost like you were trying to comfort *us*. We knew instantly you were the one."

Bev and Perry rarely alluded to Julie's adoption. They talked about it infrequently enough while Julie was growing up that she almost forgot she was adopted. Sometimes it was a strange jolt to be reminded of the fact.

"I'm sure I was smiling because I knew too," replied Julie, and she meant it. Through the years she was intermittently curious about whom her biological parents might be, but never dwelled on it. She long ago decided she did not much care to ever find them because Bev and Perry were the only parents she knew. And she would not want it any other way.

Julie put her arm around Bev's shoulders for a squeeze.

"Have you heard anymore from Mike Hughes?" asked Bev, abruptly changing the subject.

"Uh…no. Why?"

"Oh, just wondering," replied Bev with a grin.

Julie was not exactly sure why Bev was *wondering*. But she knew the questioning was not innocuous coming from her mom.

"Your dad's thinking about hiring him for this Harriet lawsuit," continued Bev. "Maybe you two could get together sometime."

Julie glanced at Bev with a raised eyebrow. Julie was unaccustomed to her mom being *that* overt in nudging her toward potential romance.

Bev rounded out her pitch with, "He was always such a nice boy."

"He's a widower with four kids now," protested Julie. She was struck by their peculiar role reversal—she was used to her mom being the voice of reason in these situations. "Besides, if he's going to be our lawyer, wouldn't that be like a conflict of interest or something?"

"I don't know about that. Just something for you to think about, maybe."

Julie kissed Bev's cheek. "You're a good mom."

Together, they stepped out of the cold, quiet night, back into the warm glow and sweet aromas of the kitchen, and into the hearty embrace of their family's laughter and love.

Chapter 11

Overnight, several inches of snow and a generous helping of new ice coated Cedar Springs. It was enough to close area schools for the day. But for the Shellys it meant scraping windshields and leaving home earlier than usual to navigate the glazed road on the way to the SB&C. Julie and Bev rode together in Julie's car, picking up Bonnie on their way to the café.

Just before seven o'clock, Hugh and Robyn stopped by the café on their way out of town to hug everyone goodbye. From there they would drive their rental car back to Charlotte, then catch a flight home to Jacksonville, Florida. Julie loved having her brother around and his departure left her feeling unusually melancholy for the rest of the gray, overcast morning.

Early that afternoon, Julie's holiday spirit regained its footing as she prepared for a new mission. The sun barely pierced the dense clouds as she exited the back of the café carrying a gift basket of baked goods toward her car. Beth pulled her police cruiser into the café's meager parking lot, rolled down her window, and stopped beside Julie's car.

"Hey! You didn't get a snow day today?"

"Nope," replied Beth. "Can you believe it? The public expects us to keep them safe, even when it snows. Where are you headed?"

"Out on a limb," said Julie playfully.

"Huh?"

"Just taking some goodies over to Mike's house."

"You're taking your goodies *where*?" teased Beth.

"Stop. I gotta go before I chicken out."

"Wait, did he invite you over?"

"Uh, no. That's the out-on-a-limb part."

"But how does the movie connection thing work if you're trying to force it instead of just letting it happen?"

"What?"

"Come on, that's what George does in the movie! Remember? He shows up at Mary's house uninvited and they end up making out and honeymooning in the leaky old house and having a bunch of babies. So, are you *sure* you're ready for this?"

"Hey, I'm not trying to force any connections. In fact, I'm really trying to forget about all this movie coincidence nonsense. I'm just taking the man some croissants. No big deal."

"Uh, huh," said Beth with a very suspicious grin. "Well, do you need an official police escort?"

Julie rolled her eyes and set the basket in the front passenger seat of her car. "I don't think that would be a wise use of taxpayer money."

"I don't know about that. There's a lot of taxpayers who'd support a move like this."

Before Julie's excursion to Mike's house, she drove the short distance home to check on Perry. She found him sitting in his recliner, semi-watching an afternoon talk show on TV. She could tell he was exhausted with being homebound.

"Hey, Dad. How're you feeling?"

"Oh, fine. Just fine. Pretty good, really."

"Tired of TV yet?"

"I was tired of TV three days ago. I've been reading quite a bit. Just taking a break."

"Good. Do you need anything? Can I make you some tea?"

"That'd be great. Thank you."

Julie entered the kitchen and found the tin of Perry's favorite cinnamon tea. She filled the kettle and set it on the stove to boil. As she waited for the water, she pondered how she had never seen her dad look frail before. It was startling—she never really thought he seemed that old. He was definitely on the mend, but the heart attack had exacted a toll and she feared he would never be the same again.

The water boiled and she made his cup of tea, with a dash of sugar stirred in, just the way he liked it. She walked the mug into the living room where Perry's eyelids looked heavy. She set the mug on the lamp table beside him and he smiled warmly at her.

"Thank you, dear."

"You're welcome." She kissed him on the cheek. "I'll be back to check on you later, okay?"

He patted her arm and Julie returned to her frigid car. As Julie turned back onto Main Street, she was suddenly hampered by second thoughts about her trip to Mike's house. Her stop at home and rumination about her dad's mortality slowed the momentum of her mission. Perhaps Beth was right—maybe she *was* forcing things a bit. Despite her misgivings, she coerced herself to press on toward the old Gilroy house.

❋ ❋ ❋

Julie inhaled deeply and exhaled very slowly in an attempt to ward off the butterflies swarming her insides as she strolled up the cracked sidewalk and steps leading from the curb to Mike's front door. She took another deep breath before reaching out to ring the doorbell, which made a forlorn, clanking noise. Julie cringed, hoping she had not broken something or awakened a napping child. She was a millisecond from simply leaving the basket of baked goods on the porch and sprinting back to her car, when the old wooden door creaked open. Tommy, Mike's five-year-old son, stood there in his pajamas. He stared up at Julie and coughed. He was clearly under the weather and Julie cringed internally at the significant mucus visible in both his nostrils.

"Hi there, Tommy. Yikes! Sounds like you're fighting a cold," she offered cheerfully.

Julie heard Mike's mother, Sarah, call from the top of the stairs, "Tommy, who's at the door?"

He yelled back, "I forgot her name!"

"It's Julie Shelly," said Julie quietly. She grinned at Tommy, but he just stared at the basket in her hands.

Sounds of considerable coughing and other child commotion emanated from the house. Tommy disappeared back inside, without relaying the message of Julie's identity to the proper authorities. Julie remained awkwardly on the doorstep, calculating her next move. She was about to slip away again when Mike appeared in the doorway. His hair was bedraggled, his face unshaven and he wore his bathrobe. His eyes were puffy, and his nose was red as if he just stepped out of a cold medicine commercial. Julie was a bit surprised to see him. She was unfamiliar with his work schedule but anticipated she would likely have to leave the basket of goodies with Mike's mother.

"Julie! What are you doing here?" asked Mike in a non-accusatory manner. He turned to yell upstairs, "It's Julie Shelly, Mom!" The exertion triggered an unflattering coughing fit in Mike that raged for several seconds as Julie silently cursed her wretched spontaneity.

"What's *she* doing here?" Julie heard Sarah reply. Julie did not detect warm vibes from Mike's mother.

Mike looked exasperated after recovering from his cough. "Sorry. It's crazy around here today." He suddenly doubled over with another deep coughing spasm that seemed to shave a year off his lifespan. Julie was unsure whether she should pat his back, or perhaps call 911. Instead, she winced sympathetically while the cough ran its course. When he finally came up for air he said, "Oh man. Excuse me. I'm kind of battling a cough thing."

"I'm sorry. I really should've called first. I just wanted to bring by some stuff from the café. I thought the kids might, you know, enjoy loading up on carbs. And maybe you too. And your mom." She immediately thought it sounded like a lame explanation, particularly the insinuation that his mother might want to binge on baked goods. However, she tried to mask her insecurity by smiling.

"Oh, thanks a lot!" said Mike as she handed him the basket. Tommy swiftly reappeared and lifted the basket's lid, pulling out a chocolate chip muffin. Mike just as swiftly swiped it from Tommy's hands.

"Mike!" called Sarah from upstairs, "Janie's calling you! Will you see what she needs? I'm helping Zuzu."

"Sorry, we've got a houseful of sick kids today," explained Mike, "so I need to…"

"Oh, sure. Like I said, sorry I didn't call first. Do you need any help?"

A phone rang. Mike was quite distracted by all the kid chaos. Tommy reappeared again and tugged on the basket. Mike set the basket on the floor and headed to the stairs. Seeing his opportunity, Tommy's eyes lit up and he quickly grabbed the muffin he selected earlier and took a huge bite out of it, careful not to make eye contact with Julie.

The phone continued ringing.

"Uh, would you mind answering that?" asked Mike from halfway up the stairs. "Sorry, I'm not sure where my phone is."

"Sure!" replied Julie, quickly reasoning that her outing was already going off the rails, so she might as well embrace the bizarreness. She began a living room hunt, following the ring tone to the couch where she located the cell phone hidden between cushions. She retrieved it and answered, "Hello?"

"Hi! Is Mike there?" asked a hurried-sounding female with a profound Southern accent.

"Uh, yes, but he's kind of busy right now. Can I take a message?"

"Is this Julie Shelly?"

"Yes," replied Julie hesitantly, and curiously.

"Hey! It's Sandy!"

Julie was instantly embarrassed for initially failing to recognize Sandy Wilson's voice on the phone.

"Oh, hey Sandy!" Julie hoped she sounded enthusiastic enough, but the loud household chaos proved quite distracting. She was not sure whether she should try to stop Tommy who had already moved on from the half-eaten muffin to a croissant.

"Sorry, uh, I'm confused—why are you answering Mike's phone?" inquired Sandy good-naturedly.

Julie thought it was a rather nosy question, but knew Sandy meant no harm. "That is a good question, actually."

"Never mind. None of my biz anyway. Unless you've got your eye on Mike, let me know, because if so, I'll keep shopping for a lawyer. Know what I mean?" Sandy laughed at herself.

"Not really," replied Julie, a bit bewildered by the strange turn in her Tuesday afternoon.

"Okay, tell Mike I'll be in town again next weekend. Wanted to see if he's available Saturday night to go over some legal docs."

Julie thought a Saturday night was an odd time to pore over "legal docs," but this was Sandy and Sandy did things the Sandy way. "Got it. I'll pass that along."

"Great! You take care then, Julie."

"You too. Bye." Julie set the phone on the coffee table in front of the couch.

The household decibel level reached new heights with one of the children upstairs now crying, while another yelled for Mike. Julie located a pad of sticky notes and a pen on the dining room table, jotted Sandy's message on a note, and stuck it on Mike's phone.

She started to announce her imminent departure but thought better of yelling "bye" and simply headed toward the front door. But then she noticed Tommy setting his half-eaten croissant on a couch cushion. He reached in the basket and pulled out another muffin, but Julie stepped over just in time to intercept it.

"Sorry, but I think your dad wants you to save some for later," she said in her friendliest babysitter voice. She knelt beside him to replace the muffin in the basket. She smiled at Tommy who suddenly and uncontrollably sneezed in her face from point-blank range. Julie felt a small blob of projectile mucus clinging to her left cheek. She closed her eyes, momentarily stunned and decidedly grossed out. She slowly cracked open her eyes and scanned the living room for a tissue box, but finding none, she proceeded to the kitchen and located a paper towel instead.

As Julie disinfected her face, Sarah descended the stairs and took over policing Tommy away from the baked goods. After the ill children initially summoned him upstairs, Mike did not make another appearance downstairs. So, Julie politely bid goodbye to Sarah and fled the awkwardness out the front door without saying bye to Mike.

Julie was relieved to return to work where she tried to forget about her ill-fated attempt to connect with Mike. *What had she hoped would result from her gesture? A date? Marriage proposal?* The notion already seemed rather foolish to her.

✳ ✳ ✳

Late in the afternoon, Van swooped into the café as he typically did at least once a week after school hours. He was earlier than usual since school was canceled due to the snow and ice. He bounded up to the counter brimming with his typical enthusiasm.

"Yo, Jules! You weren't answering your phone earlier, so I thought I'd drop in and make this a personal invite."

"You don't say," replied Julie dryly.

"I *do* say. Now what do *you* say about me making good on my long-standing offer to take you *Van-sledding*? I'm taking some of the youth group kids from church right now."

"You offered to take me *Van-sledding*?" Julie was teasing now. She produced an abundance of excuses over the past couple years to avoid going "Van-sledding" with Van, which she always thought sounded considerably dangerous, and possibly homicidal. But he swore by it, persisted with his invitation, and she was running out of excuses not to accept.

"Yeah, I mean, only every time it snowed for the past five years. Hey, I'm just trying to broaden your horizons a little, let you in on the best-kept secret in winter sports."

"Oh, it's an official winter sport now?"

"It's in beta testing, thingamajig mode. They're thinking about adding it to the Olympics."

"Impressive. I wasn't aware. I don't know, I've got work to do."

Van glanced skeptically around the café. There were only three other people—two ladies conversing on one of the couches, and one middle-aged man huddled over his laptop at a table.

"I've got it covered," said Bonnie who was eavesdropping.

"Boom! Excuses demolished," he said.

Julie scoffed at him slightly. He drove an extremely hard bargain.

"Trust me," he continued, "whatever else you were going to do today will not even approach this in fun-ness."

Julie smiled, rolled her eyes, and finally relented. She was never in the habit of abandoning the SB&C. Over the years, her work ethic was a key ingredient in saving so much money toward her travel goal. But she checked with her mom in the kitchen who was adamant that Julie deserved a break. Of course, going Van-sledding was not the kind of activity Julie would have selected for any planned time off, but she had already committed and could not bail on Van now.

Chapter 12

In all likelihood, Van was not the inventor of "Van-sledding" but he was surely its most ardent apologist. Over the past few years, his proclivity for it spread among the youth in his sphere of influence at church and school, and they eagerly adopted his moniker for the activity. He named it after himself, joking to Julie that it was his prerogative to do so, just as "Bob" apparently had when he invented bobsledding. Van's outright goofiness often amused Julie in spite of herself.

Van-sledding entailed taking an old, detached car hood and flipping it upside down so that the smooth side lay on the snow. Using a combination of chain and ski rope, the hood was then attached to the bumper of Van's jeep. Proper Van-sledding conditions required a wide-open, snow-covered field. Van would drive the jeep through the snowy field, pulling the car hood behind it. Two or three hearty passengers would lay prone on the hood, sliding, screaming, and laughing all the way as spraying snow stung their faces. One's "turn" was over when you were either unable to hold on any longer, or unable to further tolerate the pain of the frequent slams, jolts, and shimmies of the hood bumping along the ground, and you finally rolled off the hood into the snow.

Van and his protégés from the church's youth group and his high school soccer team tried various methods of attaching padding to the hood. None worked particularly well, but any padding

was better than nothing. Mostly, the successful Van-sledder simply layered oneself in winter wear and expected plenty of bumps
and bruises along with the fun. Pain was a given and screams
were plentiful. Van-sledding was not for the faint of heart.

Van explained the ins and outs of Van-sledding to Julie on
the way to the Scotts' farm located a couple of miles outside Cedar Springs. The Scotts were lifelong members of Cedar Springs
Community Church, and grandparents of seventeen-year-old
Brandon, one of the afternoon's Van-sled enthusiasts (or gluttons
for punishment, depending on whom you asked).

For most of the afternoon's remaining sunlight, Julie rode
shotgun as Van drove his roaring jeep through the Scotts' snowy
cow pastures at often-questionable speeds, cackling and talking
over the pop Christmas tunes blaring from the jeep's radio. Van
rarely got to take a turn on the "sled" of course, since it was his
jeep and he certainly was not inclined to let any of the teenagers slide behind the wheel even if they had a driver's license.
Besides, Van had been the sled driver for several years now,
which made him the de facto expert in navigating the snow and
keeping the sledders from perishing prematurely. For Van, the
driving and frequent skidding through the snow comprised the
bulk of the merriment anyway. Julie could not help but be sucked
into the fun through his infectious enthusiasm. She laughed,
gasped, and held on for dear life. It was a welcome distraction
from the oddness of the past week and helped her shed the re-
sidual embarrassment from her delivery to Mike's house earlier
that afternoon.

After the group of eight teenagers enjoyed multiple turns
each, Van finally convinced Julie to have a go. In her first round,
she lasted barely thirty seconds on the hood. Her second round

lasted nearly a minute and introduced her to the jarring pain of Van-sledding. Her ribs seemed to absorb every bump along the route and the ungainly, involuntary dismount from the hood approximated what she imagined it must feel like to leap from a moving train. After her third round she wondered whether she had cracked multiple bones and decided a return to the jeep's passenger seat was overdue. At least she could now say she gave Van's official winter "sport" a thorough trial.

"Ready to try driving?" offered Van as Julie trudged through the snow toward the jeep. It was dusk, but his enthusiasm showed no sign of waning even after ninety minutes of Van-sledding.

"I don't know about that," replied Julie with skepticism to spare.

"Come on, it's easy. Besides, I rarely have a chance to get my sled on because I'm always driving. Just one round?"

Julie grimaced and studied his face for a moment. "Okay. *One* round." She held up her right index finger for emphasis.

Van clapped his hands and hopped out of the jeep with the engine still running. Julie took his place behind the wheel. One of the teenage girls, Mackenzie, climbed into the passenger seat to join Julie.

Julie leaned out the window toward Van, "Hey, where do I go?" she asked.

"Wherever you want!" he replied.

Van jogged through the snow toward the hood, pausing to yell back at Julie, "Try to stay away from that small rise over there though," he gestured to their right, toward a distant section of the pasture. "It slopes down to a pond on the other side."

"Okay, got it!" yelled Julie over the engine noise.

Once Van was all set on the hood, he gave Julie thumbs up and she eased her foot down on the accelerator. She had never driven on that much snow before and found it a little unnerving. After a couple minutes of puttering around the pasture, Van clearly had no trouble hanging onto the sled at Julie's geriatric speed. In between throwing snowballs, the other teens watched from a distance, amused at the kiddy ride to which Julie was subjecting Van. Finally, he wildly waved his left arm in a forward motion, which Julie glimpsed in her side-view mirror.

"I think he wants me to speed up," she remarked to Mackenzie.

Mackenzie peered out the dingy plastic back window of the jeep's canvas covering to confirm. "Yeah, I think so."

Julie ventured more pressure on the gas pedal, and quickly felt further out of control. Van loved the increased speed however, letting out a loud, long, "Woo-hoo!" as they zipped past the other seven teenagers.

Despite the flying snow, Julie caught glimpses of Van's huge smile in the side-view mirror, which made her giggle. It also made her less shy of the accelerator. She sped up some more, but Van held tight. His ride had definitely turned into the longest of the day. Julie sped up even more and the hood caught some air as it slid over a bump in the pasture. Van managed to hold on, but his smile downgraded to a subtle shade of panic as Julie showed no sign of slowing down.

Julie checked her mirror again and for a fleeting moment thought Van might be yelling something. But she could not hear him and since random yelling in a recreational context was typical of Van, she plowed ahead. She was having fun now, even feeling less alarmed by the jeep's short skids in the snow. She had inadvertently veered toward the area of the pasture Van had cautioned her to avoid. Suddenly, she glimpsed Van in the mirror gesturing wildly with one arm and it took a moment for it to dawn on her that he might be encouraging her to steer to the right.

But it was already too late.

Mackenzie recognized the approaching pond bank before Julie, and suddenly blurted out, "Watch out, that's the pond!"

Julie stepped on the brake and yanked the steering wheel to the right, but the suddenness of her overcompensation caused the jeep to drift sharply. Julie and Mackenzie screamed. The hood did not have time to change directions with the jeep, so it continued racing up the small slope that led to the pond. Van finally lost his grip, flying off the hood and over the short incline. He landed on the downside of the slope, his momentum skimming him several yards across the snowy bank, then onto the mostly ice-covered surface of the pond.

The jeep finally skidded to a stop, without flipping. Julie threw it into park, but left the engine running. She and Mackenzie unbuckled their seatbelts and scrambled out of the jeep, sprinting as fast as they could over the small snow-covered slope and down toward the pond. As they slid down the short incline, the ice underneath Van began to crack.

Julie flung herself onto the bank, lunging toward Van as far as she could without falling through ice herself. Just as the ice fully fell away under Van's weight, he latched on to Julie's outstretched hands with his. Mackenzie grabbed Julie's legs as an extra anchor.

Van fell through the ice, and he gasped at the sudden surge of freezing water jabbing him from the torso down. Julie managed to maintain her grip on his hands, but she felt his gloves slipping. Julie and Mackenzie pulled with all their strength, finally hauling him out of the water enough so he could flop himself the rest of the way onto the bank.

Van groaned and shivered uncontrollably. Julie quickly pulled Van up to a sitting position, removed her coat, and put it around him. Mackenzie added her coat as well. All three of them were wide-eyed and breathing heavily. But as their initial panic subsided, they began laughing uncontrollably.

Chapter 13

The teenagers quickly unhooked the hood from the jeep and Julie drove Van back toward town with the jeep's heater on full blast. She would have taken him straight to his house, but the SB&C and its large fireplace was much closer. When she offered that as an option, Van nodded his head vigorously and gave her a quivering thumbs up.

Van's shivering, and the sound of his chattering teeth, deepened Julie's guilt for launching him into the frozen pond. She tried to encourage him with assurance of unlimited hot beverages at the café, but knew it was rather trite comfort in the moment.

"Uh, Julie, I've got some bad news," started Van.

"What?" she replied, mildly panicked that he was going to require a trip to the emergency room instead.

"I'm afraid I'm going to have to cut you from the Olympic Van-sledding team."

She shook her head at him, chuckling. "Too soon."

It was after dark and Shelly's had already closed by the time they arrived. Julie let them in through the back door, quickly turned on the gas fireplace, and hurried to the kitchen, where she knew the cold-natured Aunt Bonnie kept a fleece blanket in a closet for days like this. In short order, Van sat in front of the fire, wrapped tightly in the blanket, with a large mug of welcome hot coffee in his hands. After she arranged his socks and sneakers close to the fire to dry, Julie pulled up a chair beside him with her own cup of coffee.

"Believe it or not, that wasn't my first time to fall through ice," said Van. "My third, actually."

Julie chuckled. "What? Seriously?"

"Yeah, there was the failed ice-fishing attempt with my dad when I was six. An ill-fated hockey game when I was fourteen. And now, tossed from a hood by an insane driver."

"I am *so* sorry!" said Julie.

"Well, at least you pulled me out, so…"

They paused to sip their drinks.

"Yeah, want to know something weird about that?"

"Maybe," he teased.

"Ever since I watched *It's a Wonderful Life* on Thanksgiving, all these random things keep happening to me sort of like stuff that happened to George Bailey in the movie."

"Whaaat? That *is* weird," he conceded. "Like what kind of stuff?"

"You know, like George rescuing his brother from the ice, except you're not my brother, so…"

"But you were adopted, so how do you know I'm *not* your brother? Maybe your life's really *Star Wars* and you're like, *Leia*. And I'm *Luke*. Plus, George didn't try to drown his brother like you did to me."

"Whatever. I know it's silly, but if you knew the extent of the coincidences, believe me, it raises the eyebrows."

"Well, a lot of people believe dumber things."

"I know. It does sound dumb."

"I didn't mean to imply dumbness."

"No, it's fine. I know it's ridiculous." She sighed and took another sip of her coffee. "At first, I thought maybe it all could mean something, like maybe it was going to bring me some clarity. Maybe give some insight about how my life has turned out so far."

He looked at her quizzically.

"Sorry," said Julie, suddenly flustered. "This probably doesn't make any sense. I know I have a great life here. And I'm totally grateful for it. It's just…there's a lot of world out there and I've barely seen any of it. Plenty in books and on TV, but not much in real life. I just want to stretch a little. That's natural, right?"

"Absolutely." He looked at the floor as he said it and she thought she detected a hint of disappointment in the way he pressed his lips together.

"Anyway, that movie stuff is probably nothing. I mean, the Mike Hughes part sure seems like a dead end."

"So, you two aren't like a couple now?"

"Not by a long shot."

"That's good to know."

She glanced at him, startled by his statement. He stared into his coffee mug, suddenly unable to make eye contact.

"Why? Were you *jealous* or something?" she asked in a teasing tone, though she was not sure she selected the right tone.

"Come on, Julie. You know I've liked you for a long time, right?"

The conversation had veered into uncomfortable territory for Julie. She suddenly had the same, sinking, butterfly feeling she had that afternoon on the way to Mike's house. Finally, she answered, "Sure. As friends though, right?"

"Well yeah, but…I like you more than that."

"You do?" she asked with raised eyebrows.

"Yeah. I don't ask just any ol' girl to go Van-sledding." He paused briefly then blurted, "I've been in love with you for a while now."

Her eyes widened. "You have?"

"Yes."

She abruptly stood and returned her chair to a nearby table. "Umm…I don't know what to say to that."

"Well, in an ideal scenario, you would say something along the lines of how you love me too, and that you would definitely like to be my exclusive girlfriend." She knew him well enough to know he couldn't help himself—his default was silly in uncomfortable moments.

She set her mug on the table and sighed in deflated fashion. "Oh, no, Van. I just…I really didn't know you felt this way. I mean, I like you too, of course. But I've been planning to leave Cedar Springs since high school, and I finally have the chance to do it soon. I'm just not really in the place for a relationship right now. It just doesn't really make sense. Know what I mean?"

He resumed staring into his coffee mug. "I suppose." She could tell by his stilted grin that he found it difficult to mask his disappointment. He stood, set his mug on the fireplace, and hung the blanket on the back of a chair. He grabbed his shoes and hurriedly slipped them on his feet without donning his damp socks.

"Well, thanks again for saving my life," he said, trying to reignite his usual humor, though it was a futile attempt.

"You're welcome," she replied, "Any time."

"So, I guess I'll see you around," he said, walking briskly toward the front door. The squeak of his wet shoes on the hardwood floor added insult to his injury. Naturally, the front door was locked, thus foiling his already clumsy escape attempt. He fumbled with the locks, but in his flustered state, could not complete the task.

Julie hurriedly crossed the café. "Sorry about that," she said, unlocking the door as quickly as possible. She held the door open for him and said, "Good night."

"Bye," he said in a clipped, defeated manner on his way out.

Julie relocked the front door and watched him rush down the sidewalk. She suddenly remembered they parked his jeep in the back and was about to step outside to remind him, but then assumed he knew what he was doing as she watched him turn right at the corner of the building at the end of the block.

Julie extinguished the fireplace, then carried their empty mugs to the kitchen and put them in the dishwasher. She locked the back door and walked to her car, replaying the exchange with Van in her mind. She felt miserable for hurting his feelings, yet she was also irritated that he suddenly complicated their comfortable friendship by bringing up his being in love with her. Then she was annoyed at herself for feeling irritated. *How could she be irritated at him for loving her?* She let her mind wander momentarily to being married to Van, but the concept simply failed to coalesce with her exotic travel future. He was a high school English teacher and coach—perfectly fine, just rather run-of-the-mill. Her whole life had been run-of-the-mill, and she was looking forward to reversing that trend. The harsh reality was Van just did not fit in with her lofty dreams.

As she pulled into her driveway, her thoughts shifted back to the afternoon's turn of events and Van's falling through the ice. She shook her head, marveling at yet another peculiar coincidence between her life and the quite fictional George Bailey's. Just when she thought she was moving on from the movie madness, it was tossed back in her face. Surely, she was reading entirely too much into recent events. She felt further irritated with herself, paranoid as to why she would project significance onto seemingly random occurrences where there was none. She protested to herself that she had not been reading into things, that these events simply happened to her. She took her key out of the ignition and said a quick, silent prayer that God would either make it all stop or make it very clear if she was actually supposed to be learning something from any of this.

She wearily climbed the stairs to her flat, entered, and dropped her keys on the lamp stand beside the couch. Then she went straight to her bedroom, donned her preferred t-shirt-and-shorts pajamas, and finally fell into bed, irked and exhausted.

Chapter 14

A full week passed after Julie and Van's ice-pond adventure. One week made a world of difference in Julie's outlook. No more weird *Wonderful Life* coincidences hounded her. She did not see Van all week either, which was quite rare, though she was afraid he had deliberately ensured their paths did not cross after their conversation at the café. The brightest aspect of the week was Perry returning to work at the SB&C on a limited basis. He even felt good enough to hire Mike to defend him against Harriet's lawsuit. Perry and Mike met several times throughout the week to go over details in preparation for the preliminary court hearing on December 12th.

When the day of the preliminary hearing arrived, neither Bev nor Aunt Bonnie was inclined to attend, knowing they would have to endure Harriet's irrational and protracted testimony on the evils of the Shelly lights extravaganza. Plus, someone had to keep the café running. So, the two of them minded the shop while Perry and Julie went to the county courthouse just three blocks west of Shelly's.

Julie certainly wanted to support her father, but she was also curious to see Mike in action as their lawyer. She took a seat in the courtroom's mostly empty gallery, while Perry sat beside Mike at the defense table. Though they had been through this court routine with Harriet before, familiarity failed to diminish Julie's nervousness during the experience.

Once the proceeding began, Harriet paced slowly, with the dramatic aid of her cane, as she addressed Judge Florence Goodrich. Judge Goodrich was a bantamweight woman in her mid-fifties with a commanding voice that belied her slight stature. She wore reading glasses that defied gravity by somehow clinging to the end of her nose. She wound her graying hair in a flawlessly tight bun that seemed to provide a natural facelift. This was the Shellys' first time in the courtroom with Judge Goodrich presiding and her demeanor instantly intimidated Julie.

Harriet droned on, frequently gesturing at a pie chart set up on an easel, as if the day's event was already the actual trial and she was Matlock. Julie wondered to whom and how much Harriet paid to have such a fancy pie chart designed. *There was no way Harriet made it herself,* she thought.

"As you can see, the number of cars driving through the downtown area of Cedar Springs rises dramatically during the first three weeks of December every year, which causes all Cedar Springs traffic to slow to a crawl. It's not even a crawl really. It's worse. It affects pretty much every aspect of life in the town during the busiest four weeks of the year," Harriet complained to the judge. "Nobody can get anything done because of all these out-of-town folks flooding in here, clogging up our roads, probably littering our streets. Driving way too slow, gawking at the lights like they own the place. The noise pollution alone is criminal."

Julie saw Mike glance at Perry with an amused look. Perry could not resist rolling his eyes.

"I've been late to, or have missed, multiple appointments over the years because of the Shellys' lights. Gas mileage is negatively affected for everyone. You take an already stressful season, add the noise, the crowds, and the insanity of the lights, and you have a recipe for serious health problems. This is the direct result of the Shelly Christmas lights display," continued Harriet, "a ridiculous mess that's been ruining the health of Cedar Springs folks for over sixty years. Not to mention my own health and sanity. It's just an awful public nuisance and it's way past time to shut it down. And furthermore…"

"Okay, Ms. Paddock, I think I get the picture," interrupted Judge Goodrich. "Why don't you save something for the actual trial? It's lunchtime and I'm getting *hangry*."

Julie glanced around with a quizzical expression, wondering if anyone else heard the judge say she was "hangry."

Mike quickly stood. "Wait, your Honor…you're not actually thinking about taking this preposterous case to trial, are you?"

"I was, actually," replied Judge Goodrich.

"But your Honor, this is a completely frivolous suit, obviously driven more by Ms. Paddock's apparent distaste for Christmas and some kind of unwarranted personal vendetta against Mr. Shelly, than anything to do with being a legitimate 'public nuisance.' The public loves the Shellys' lights display, as evidenced by the dozens of volunteers who help put up the display every year. It's a Cedar Springs institution. In fact, if she tried embracing the holiday spirit for a change, she might be surprised how much she might enjoy the lights and what they contribute to the holiday season here."

"I object!" cried Harriet, looking at Judge Goodrich. "Can I object?"

Judge Goodrich held up her hand toward Harriet and addressed Mike. "I'm not sure I would go with the Christmas-hater strategy, Mr. Hughes, but it's your defense. We will reconvene one week from today for the start of the trial."

Judge Goodrich pounded her gavel once and adjourned the hearing. Julie glanced around again at the few other faces in the gallery to see whether anyone else looked as stunned as she felt. No one did.

✳ ✳ ✳

Julie waited for Perry in the hallway outside the courtroom. When Mike and Perry finally emerged, Mike greeted Julie with an enthusiastic "Hi!" along with a brief hug. Considering their last interaction at his house the previous week, Julie was a little surprised by how glad Mike seemed to see her.

"Are your kids feeling better?" asked Julie.

"Much better. Thanks for asking. By the way, I'm really sorry about the other day. I just wanted to apologize. That was some ugly chaos."

"It was no big deal," she said. "Don't worry about it."

"No, I felt bad leaving you hanging. I didn't even thank you properly for bringing all those goodies. Which were fantastic by the way."

"I'm glad you enjoyed them."

"Can I make it up to you with lunch or something?"

Julie was taken aback that he was asking her out in front of her dad. Assuming it was really a date. *Was it*? She was suddenly flooded with doubt. "Uh…sure," she managed. "But don't feel like you owe me or anything."

"Where should we go? Your pick."

Julie risked a glance at Perry who mischievously raised his eyebrows at her. She grinned—it was good to see his sense of humor returning.

Julie generally disliked selecting restaurants. She typically deferred to the opinion of others since she usually found something satisfactory on the menu almost anywhere. At Mike's insistence, however, she finally selected Ancelloti's, a small Italian restaurant near the courthouse. She invited Perry to join them, but he declined, claiming fatigue and a desire to head home. She knew better, though—Perry was excusing himself to ensure this materialized as a *date*, but Julie did not protest.

✳ ✳ ✳

Inside Ancelloti's, Julie and Mike sat across from each other at a small table along the back wall of the restaurant. Julie enjoyed a bowl of minestrone, while Mike ate lasagna. He peppered her with questions about her world travel plans.

"I think I'm going to spend the first month touring England, Scotland, Ireland, and Wales. Then I'm hopping over to France. From there, Scandinavia."

"Oslo?" he asked.

"Probably. I haven't completely mapped out the Scandinavian leg yet."

She took a sip of her soup and glanced at the restaurant entrance just as Van strolled in. He immediately saw Julie and managed a slight wave, though she knew him well enough to detect the hesitance in his body language, which she read as him debating whether to turn around and walk out.

"I've actually been to Oslo," said Mike, oblivious to Van's entrance. "Really cool city."

She watched Van pay for a take-out order at the counter. Van took his plastic bag with Styrofoam container and left without looking back in Julie's direction, which disappointed her. It surely meant he was still upset about their post ice-plunge conversation at the café.

"I went on this boat tour of the fjords in Norway. You've *got* to do that while you're there. I'll try to find the name of the tour company. So beautiful. I've never seen anything like it," droned Mike. Julie missed most of his Norwegian travel tips, distracted as she was by Van's cameo.

"I'm sorry," interrupted Julie, "will you excuse me for a second? I'll be right back."

She hurried to the parking lot outside the restaurant where Van was almost to his jeep.

"Van! Wait up!"

He paused with the jeep door open as Julie approached.

"I thought you said a relationship doesn't make sense for you right now. Since you're leaving town so soon and all."

She had rarely seen Van upset. "It's not like that. Mike's working on this case for my dad and he just invited me to lunch."

"Well, enjoy your lunch. I'm late for class." He abruptly shut the jeep door.

"Van, come on, please!"

He quickly rolled down his window. "It's really fine, Julie. I'm sorry, I've gotta go." He started the engine, backed quickly out of the parking space, and drove away.

Julie exhaled deeply, hung her head, then returned inside the restaurant to her now-cold minestrone and more of Mike's warmed-over European memories.

Chapter 15

The morning after the preliminary court hearing and Julie's quasi-date at Ancelotti's, the SB&C bustled with its usual crowd. Between the customer load and her inopportune interaction with Van the previous afternoon, Julie felt unusually stressed. So, she was grateful for the oasis of seeing two friendly faces when Beth and Eric entered the café together and sat in the last two empty counter stools.

"Okay, Julie, last night, it was so weird. I just felt compelled, I couldn't figure out why, but I found myself running through downtown, just randomly yelling out, 'Merry Christmas, courthouse! Merry Christmas, you wonderful old pharmacy!' So, what do you think that means?" Eric grinned, appearing quite pleased with himself for his opening zinger.

Julie smirked as she filled two mugs with coffee and gently slid them across the counter to Beth and Eric.

"He's not funny anymore," remarked Julie to Beth.

"Only every once in a while," said Beth, patting Eric's arm.

"So, what part's coming up next for ya, Georgie?" continued Eric.

"The part where I realize there is absolutely nothing to any of this silly stuff and I forget all about it," replied Julie, hoping he would take the hint that she was not particularly in the mood to be harassed about the movie at the moment.

"Oh, good. So, you're not really crazy?" asked Eric, clearly not taking the hint.

"Okay, you're really *not* funny anymore," said Beth, taking up for Julie.

One of the town's postal workers, Alan Hackett, entered the café and approached the counter. Alan was a fixture in Cedar Springs—someone Julie, Beth, and Eric had known forever, without ever really knowing much about him. The fifty-year-old had been a postman for over twenty years, but it was unusual to see him enter the SB&C carrying mail, since he normally placed it in the mailbox by the entrance to the parking lot behind the café.

"Good morning, Alan," said Julie cheerfully.

"Morning, Julie."

"Can I pour you a cup?"

"Oh, no, that's all right. Appreciate it. Got your mail here…" Alan set a small bundle of mail on the counter in front of Julie. "But I had to hand you this piece myself." He held up a severely tattered envelope that looked like it might have been white at one point and passed it to Julie. "It's really been through the wringer," continued Alan, "but look, the strange thing is, check out the postmark."

Julie examined the front of the envelope, which contained multiple postmarks on top of, and around, the postage stamp. The postage stamp design itself was a drawing of a snowy village with the word *Greetings* printed along the bottom of the stamp. The price in the upper right-hand corner of the stamp was twenty-two cents. Julie squinted, trying to make out the most legible postmark. "Does that say 1986?" asked Julie, holding out the envelope for Beth, Eric, and Alan to have a look.

"Yeah, looks like it's been lost in the mail for a while," said Alan.

Beth looked at Alan with wrinkled brow. "Y'all can lose mail for thirty years?"

Alan shrugged. "Not typically. We usually do a lot better than that. But I *have* heard of this happening before."

"I was born in '87 though," said Julie. "And Mom and Dad adopted me just before I turned one. So, no one could've mailed me anything at this address in 1986."

"Huh." Alan was stumped.

"Are you going to open it today, Sherlock, or should we wait another thirty years?" asked Eric, amused and intrigued.

Beth, Eric, and Alan leaned in a bit closer as Julie carefully opened the envelope. She pulled out a Christmas card with a photograph on the cover of the Cedar Springs steel truss bridge, covered in snow, and adorned with white Christmas lights. Julie had barely opened the card and begun silently speed-reading the handwritten message inside when Beth blurted out, "What does it say?"

Julie read the card aloud, "*December 25th, 1986. Dear Julie, You truly have the most amazing life. Thank you for giving me hope. Love, Gwen.*"

Julie looked up from the card. Everyone wore similarly baffled expressions.

"Who's Gwen?" asked Beth.

Julie's expression slowly transitioned from puzzled to annoyed as it dawned on her that this bore the hallmark of an Eric prank. She suddenly slapped Eric on the upper arm and top of his head with the card in quick succession. "You almost got me!" shouted Julie.

"What?" said Eric incredulously, though with a huge grin on his face.

"*You truly have the most amazing life?*'" Julie repeated in a mocking tone. "Nice try."

"It's not from me!" Eric protested.

"Eric..." started Beth doubtfully.

"I swear! I mean, I *wish* I'd thought of doing this. Look at this thing.... You think I have time for all this detail? It looks totally authentic! Gotta hand it to whoever did this—they went all out," marveled Eric.

Alan nodded. "Sure looks real to me."

Something suddenly occurred to Julie. "Wait a minute..." She rushed around the counter and over to the small card carousel near the cash register. The carousel held several postcards and greeting cards featuring various photos of Cedar Springs. "*We* sell these cards!" she exclaimed, holding up an identical Christmas card to the mystery card from "Gwen," each with the same photo of the Cedar Springs steel truss bridge at Christmastime.

It was Beth's turn to slap Eric on the arm.

"Babe, I swear it wasn't me!" Eric insisted.

"So how long have y'all been selling those cards?" asked Beth.

"At least thirty years apparently," said Julie, holding up the card from Gwen. "Or this Gwen bought it somewhere else."

"That, or someone's pulling your leg," said Alan.

Julie and Beth stared at Eric accusingly, but he held up his hands in innocent protest and said, "For once, I can't claim credit for this."

Bev entered from the kitchen carrying a tray of freshly baked muffins, which she transferred to the display case. Julie returned behind the counter. "Mom, do you know how long we've been selling these Christmas cards?"

Bev placed the last muffin in the case, then examined the card which Julie handed her. "I don't know, but I want to say probably around the time you were in junior high," replied Bev.

Julie was not satisfied. She assumed Bev's estimate was probably off by over a decade based on the 1986 postmark on the envelope and the fact Julie entered seventh grade in 1999.

Later that morning, Perry arrived at the café to work a few hours. He was recovering well from his heart attack and slowly increasing his daily time spent at work. Julie asked him about the card as well, but he had no idea when they started selling cards with that particular photograph on the front. Julie did not bother checking with Aunt Bonnie since she generally could not even remember what she had for breakfast that morning.

※ ※ ※

During the typical early afternoon lull in café traffic, Julie walked a few blocks north to a small, old house with a neatly kept wraparound porch. A small sign in the front yard announced the house as home of the Cedar Springs Historical Society.

Inside the house, Julie found one volunteer on duty—a seventy-year-old woman named Louise Butler who was an acquaintance of Julie's from church. Louise greeted Julie warmly, offering her a cup of hot tea, which Julie gratefully accepted. After very slowly pouring Julie a cup and adding a half teaspoon of sugar, they made small talk for a few minutes until a conversational opening finally enabled Julie to explain the reason for her spontaneous visit. She showed Louise the Christmas card and the envelope with the 1986 postmark, explaining how it had apparently been lost in the mail for over thirty years.

Louise carried the Christmas card to an antique desk, where she retrieved a magnifying glass from a drawer. Louise carefully examined the card and envelope with the magnifying glass like an archaeologist. Julie wondered if Louise really had that level of *Antiques Road Show*-like expertise. Regardless, she appreciated Louise's effort to indulge Julie's curiosity.

After a couple minutes of thorough examination, Louise said, "Hmm…well the postmark seems authentic, though it's hard to tell for sure since they're layered on top of each other like that. The earliest one sure looks like it says '1986' though. If this is a forgery, someone went to an awful lot of trouble."

Julie nodded in agreement, though she could not help but feel a little disappointed. She knew she was somewhat grasping at straws with her visit to the Historical Society, but she was so curious about the odd card she figured it was worth a try.

"I know the Reed Card Company in Asheville has been printing Christmas cards with this bridge photograph for years," continued Louise. She lowered the magnifying glass and stared at the card's bridge photo for another moment, then squinted her eyes and pursed her lips in apparent deep thought.

"What is it?" asked Julie.

"You know…I don't think the bridge has always been decorated with white lights at Christmas."

Julie raised her eyebrows. She had not considered that wrinkle. Her family's famous lights display only covered Main Street and the courthouse square. Since the steel truss bridge was on the eastern edge of downtown past where the Shelly lights ended, the city of Cedar Springs took charge of any Christmas décor on the bridge and its immediate surroundings.

Louise shuffled across the room to another antique, a wooden file cabinet, pulled out a creaky drawer, and rummaged through decrepit folders, yellowed papers, and decaying photographs.

"In fact," continued Louise, "I don't think the city started using white lights until around the mid-nineties."

Julie marveled at the capacity of people to remember such mundane, random things. Well, people besides Aunt Bonnie anyway.

Louise finally pulled a photo from a folder near the back of the drawer and held it up for Julie to see. It was a color photo of the bridge, at night, with larger green, red, and blue Christmas bulbs strung on the bridge.

"Aha! This shot is dated December 18th, 1985," said Louise, reading the writing on the back of the photo.

"Colored lights," confirmed Julie. She was impressed with Louise's relatively quick detective work.

"There you go. So, they might have switched to white lights in 1986, but I'm almost positive it wasn't until 1995 or so. Whoever 'Gwen' is, I don't know where she found a card like this in 1986. Maybe someone at the post office was asleep when they stamped that postmark."

Perhaps, thought Julie, *but it still does not explain why the inside of the card is dated 'December 25, 1986' since I wasn't even born yet.* And she didn't even live in Cedar Springs until the Shellys adopted her in 1988, so it made no sense for a Christmas card to be addressed to her nearly two years before that. Plus, there was the glaring issue that she did not know anyone named Gwen. She figured an odd prank was still the best explanation.

Julie smiled at Louise. "Well, thank you very much for your help, Louise. And thank you again for the tea. I really appreciate it."

"Sorry we couldn't completely solve the mystery for you," replied Louise.

On her walk back to the café, Julie wracked her brain for a time when she might have met a Gwen, but she came up dry. Her mind drifted back to Eric and she smiled to herself. Her suspicion returned that the mystery card was just Eric's sense of humor getting a workout.

Chapter 16

The Shellys' Christmas lights display was illuminated on the first of December, just as it had been every December first since 1948. Opening night for the lights always featured a brief ceremony, with a few welcoming remarks by Perry, followed by his pressing the button to light up the Christmas tree in the courthouse square. Perry had pressed the button every year since his father's death in 1999. Immediately after the tree was lit, he would press a second button that turned on the rest of the Main Street lights in a block-by-block domino fashion.

This year however, since Perry was not released from the hospital until December first, Bev and Julie decided to go ahead and turn on the lights as scheduled but delayed the traditional opening night ceremony and festivities until Perry felt well enough to attend. After all, Perry was present at every single opening night of the lights since he was born in 1952. No one wanted to see that streak end.

Opening night was an entrenched tradition for Cedar Springs' citizens. It served as the community's unofficial kickoff to the holiday season. It always attracted a crowd of hundreds, and downtown businesses stayed open late to capitalize. The SB&C was no exception in this regard. The Shellys made their famous Christmas cookies available to purchase for the first time during each holiday season on opening night of the lights. Perry's mother and father began selling the Christmas cookies in 1965 to coincide with the tree lighting. Their original offering consisted of traditional sugar cookies with just the right thickness of colored icing. Julie's grandfather was meticulous on that point. One of her earliest memories of the café was sitting on a wood stool beside him, absorbed in observing his method of individually spreading the icing on each cookie. He knew exactly how large a dollop should be piped onto each one. Julie would watch, mesmerized, as he hovered over a large tray, icing dozens of cookies in seconds with his machine-like precision and efficiency. She could not believe how he made each dollop virtually identical.

In the early 1980s, Perry added his personal favorite—oatmeal chocolate chip cookies—to the Shellys' Christmas cookie repertoire. Though the sugar cookies remained most popular by a slim margin, both kinds were perennially in such high demand that it was an annual stress for the Shellys to keep pace with the orders.

Since opening night was delayed for Perry's heart-attack recovery, the Shellys also postponed the availability of their Christmas cookies. Julie almost immediately second-guessed that decision as they were bombarded with constant questions and requests during the first week of December. Though her lifelong association with the SB&C should have prepared her for this maxim, she had not fully comprehended it until that year's great Christmas cookie delay: *you simply do not come between folks and their Christmas cookies.*

Once Perry returned home from the hospital and his doctor was satisfied that he was fit to resume working on a limited basis, the family rescheduled the opening night festivities for Thursday, December 13th.

The Shelly Christmas lights display was always available to the public without an admission charge. However, this year Julie suggested they solicit opening night donations for the Lighthouse Adoption Network, since its primary fundraising night was cut short by the unfortunate gym fire fiasco at Cedar Springs High School a couple of weeks prior. At Julie's suggestion, the Shellys also planned to donate all the proceeds from the SB&C's opening night Christmas cookie sales to Lighthouse.

At dusk, a dozen volunteers canvassed the courthouse square for donations, carrying plastic buckets adorned with the Lighthouse Adoption Network logo. Julie, Beth, and Eric were part of the volunteer crew. After milling through the crowd for over an hour, the trio converged for a break near the large banner strung across Main Street that read: *Shelly Family Christmas Lights Spectacular!*

Beth peppered Julie with questions, impeding Julie's attempt to put the *Wonderful Life* vagaries behind her. Julie did not like feeling annoyed with her best friend, but she was veering closer to telling Beth to give it a rest. She semi-excused Beth's interrogations, reasoning that Beth's police-officer investigative instincts were kicking in. The mysterious Christmas card particularly intrigued Beth, and while Julie conceded its inexplicability, she was growing weary of Beth's peskiness about the whole thing and did not see how the strange card and a seventy-year-old movie could possibly be related anyway.

"But think about this for a minute..." Beth persisted.

"Let's not," said Julie. "My brain hurts."

Beth ignored her friend's request. "I'm not convinced this is a prank. I mean, who else have you told about the *Wonderful Life* stuff?"

"Just you. And Eric, unfortunately." Julie glanced at Eric, who responded with raised eyebrows and an innocent shrug. "And Van."

"Van knows about this stuff?" asked Eric. "It was definitely him then."

"Believe me, it wasn't Van," said Julie, keeping to herself the fact she and Van were not currently on speaking terms. She felt a nervous wave crash in the pit of her stomach at the reminder of not seeing Van for several days. It was the longest such stretch she could remember since she'd known him. She suddenly realized she truly missed him. And it hurt. For a fleeting moment she wondered if this feeling was actually something akin to love. Her mind briefly spun with the disorienting notion.

"Your parents? Aunt Bonnie?" asked Beth.

"No and no," said Julie emphatically, snapping out of her musing about Van.

"Then you might need to accept the real possibility that you're dealing with some kind of magic Christmas card here." Beth was only half-joking.

Eric scoffed. "Did you really just say *magic Christmas card?*"

"Hey, don't you have some donations to solicit or something?" snapped Beth in good humor. She refocused on Julie. "What'd she say in the card? 'Thank you for giving me hope'? Or something like that?"

"Yeah," confirmed Julie with a weary exhale.

"Like she's met you before," continued Beth.

"I know. It's very weird. It does make me wonder."

"What?" asked Beth with excited eyes, craving any tidbit to shed light on the mystery card.

Julie already regretted letting herself be sucked back into this speculation game. She thought about pulling out of the nosedive, but her friend's eager gaze coaxed against Julie's will. "I don't know…it kind of makes me wonder if something big is supposed to happen. Like on Christmas Eve or something."

"Like what?" Beth's eyes somehow lit up even more.

Eric interjected. "Like you two get carted off to the loony bin." Julie thought his smirk betrayed that he derived a bit too much pleasure from crashing their fantasy with his dose of reality.

Beth ignored him and Julie tried to, though his comment stoked a minor fear she harbored since all this began—that she was perhaps in the early stages of going crazy. "I don't know! Maybe I'm supposed to help someone or something. Maybe discover my entire life's purpose in the process?" She tossed in the bit about her "*life's purpose*" to indicate an ironic hipness to these musings, though she secretly loved the idea of her life's real purpose becoming evident.

"I'm sorry, but people don't find out what their life's purpose is through an old card from *Gwen*," said Eric rather cynically. "Julie—you help people all the time, so you apparently inspired a Gwen at some point, and she sent you a cryptic thank you note. And some clown at the post office postmarked it with an old date. Case closed."

Beth glared at her husband and retorted, "I'm taking back your Christmas present. And I'm sticking with the magic Christmas card theory because it's way more fun."

The lights display in the square and on Main Street were dark that night just for the purpose of the ceremony. It was nearing seven o'clock, so the trio of friends paused their ongoing conversation and Julie made her way to the courthouse square, joining Bev and Perry for the official tree lighting. Aunt Bonnie remained at the café with Bev's niece, Teresa, who arrived that morning to help with the holiday rush, and to assume Julie's job once she departed on her overseas adventure.

Perry stepped up to the microphone to address the large crowd, which was enthusiastic in spite of the arctic night air. As he was about to commence speaking, Harriet drove around the square in her pickup truck. A large, white wooden sign anchored in the truck bed featured letters painted in bold black, which read: *BOYCOT SHELLY'S LIGHTS*. The other side of the sign read: *NO MORE CHRISTMAS LIGHT TRAFFIC JAMS*. Harriet drove with her window down, leaning out the window with a megaphone in her left hand. Through the megaphone she blared, over and over, "Boycott Shelly's! Boycott Shelly's!"

Julie started to shake her head in bewildered disgust, but then took her cue from her parents and did her best to ignore the interruption. It was not easy.

Most people in the crowd glanced around to identify the commotion before returning their attention to Perry. Perry's eyes followed Harriet's truck for a moment and Julie heard him let out a soft sigh. Julie leaned slightly toward Perry and said under her breath, "She misspelled *boycott*."

That made her dad grin.

The crowd seemed to sympathize with Perry, as several booed Harriet when she drove past. Julie was much more surprised by Harriet's ability to get such a large sign made and mounted in her truck than she was by Harriet's typical party pooper gesture.

"Good evening! Welcome. Thank you for being here. I'm sorry for the delay this year," began Perry into the microphone, "but hopefully you'll agree that it's better late than never. Thank you so very much for your patience and kind support of our family over the years. Thank you also for all the cards and food and generosity you've shown me the past couple weeks since my heart attack."

The crowd cheered and applauded.

"So, it is with particular excitement and thankfulness for the holidays this year, that I'm proud to declare the seventieth annual Shelly Family Christmas Lights Spectacular officially open!"

The crowd roared, while Perry surprised Julie, gesturing with his right hand for her to press the button to light the tree. He had not told her of his plan to pass the torch to her this year. She hesitated as the crowd continued cheering. Perry nodded reassuringly. He wanted her to have the honor. Julie finally stepped forward to the green button, which was mounted on a stand by the microphone, and pressed it. The tree lit up in a brilliant swirl of white lights with red accents and the crowd cheered even louder.

DJ Cal Stevens started playing Christmas music through the speakers set up around the square and Julie pressed the second button that illuminated the rest of the massive Main Street display. Every building for several blocks, on both sides of the street, was doused in strands of lights that turned Cedar Springs into a scene straight out of Santa's workshop. After the cheering faded, the crowd slowly dispersed to take in the sights and sounds, with a sizable proportion of people making a beeline toward Shelly's.

After handshakes and hugs from multiple well-wishers, Perry, Bev, and Julie pried themselves from the crowd in the courthouse square to return to the café. Julie offered to drive Perry, even though they were just a few blocks away. She was still concerned about his post-heart-attack strength, but he insisted on walking. He loved the festive opening night atmosphere. The night was the highlight of every year for him: the people thronging downtown, children reveling in the lights display, the brisk December air. Julie watched her dad taking everything in. His eyes looked tired, but his face was beaming. She slipped her arm around his and leaned her head on his shoulder, drinking in the moment to help lodge it in her memory. Their walk across the courthouse square and down Main Street to the SB&C took a much slower than usual pace. Julie knew her dad disliked this aspect of his heart attack and recovery more than anything. It was not easy for an avid cyclist, occasional jogger, and devoted baker to have to throw on the brakes like this. Yet, for that night's celebration, their pace was just right.

As they walked, Harriet continued her futile attempt to disrupt the festive atmosphere with her bullhorn. She drove repeatedly around the courthouse square, then drove up and down Main Street a few times, her voice booming out of the driver's side window as she went. The townsfolk seemed to be of one mind about ignoring her, however. Harriet's was a solo protest rally, but it grated on Julie's nerves nonetheless.

When Julie and her parents finally made it to the Shelly's storefront, they were rather shocked to find the crowd spilling out of the café and down the sidewalk in both directions. Sizable crowds and rampant Christmas cookie sales were not uncommon, but this crowd was unlike anything they had seen before. Julie looked at Perry with a mix of pleasant surprise and alarm. Beth and Eric arrived, similarly wide-eyed at the jostling crowd.

"Hate to say it, but this has all the hallmarks of a cookie run," quipped Eric.

Even though she was off-duty, Beth instinctively launched into cop mode with a section of the crowd that was growing agitated. "All right everybody, calm down! Form a line. For Pete's sake, act like you've had cookies before. Y'all are about to cause a cookie panic!"

Julie politely, and repeatedly said, "Excuse us!" as she and her parents squeezed through the crowd to the entrance. They finally squirmed inside where Bonnie and Teresa were clearly frazzled behind the counter.

Julie hurriedly followed Bonnie into the kitchen where she tied on her apron in record time. "Wow! What's going on?"

"I don't know. It's worse than ever this year!" exclaimed Bonnie. "Seems like just a handful of people are buying up most of the cookies and folks are getting ticked off. I don't think we have enough to make it through the night! People are starting to push and shove. It's getting ugly out there."

Julie thought for a second, summoned some determination, and exited the kitchen into the café on a mission. "Okay, everyone! May I have your attention?" yelled Julie. "We're very excited that you're all here and we want you to have the best experience possible. However, there's apparently some cookie hoarding going on, so we're going to ask everyone to keep their orders to a reasonable number so that we can hopefully serve everyone. We will also take orders for cookies if we sell out tonight. And keep in mind, we do have many of our famous pies available as well. Thank you!"

Perry, Bev, and Teresa smiled at Julie's chipper effort. Much of the crowd had not paid adequate attention, but it was an admirable attempt.

Immediately following her address to the crowd, Julie stepped up to the next man in line. "All right, sir, how may I help you?"

"I'll have five dozen of your Christmas sugar cookies, please," replied the man.

Julie was noticeably disheartened—the man obviously had not listened to her plea. "Five dozen? *That's* your reasonable order?" inquired Julie.

"Yeah, I was going to buy *ten* dozen. These are the best Christmas cookies around. Plus, it's for a good cause, right?" said the man, gesturing toward the sign on the countertop about the night's cookie proceeds benefitting the Lighthouse Adoption Network.

"Right, of course. We're just trying to make sure there are enough to go around tonight. How 'bout I sell you two dozen tonight and you can sign up to have the other three delivered to your house in a day or two?"

"What, you mean I'd have to wait? No thanks. Just give me five dozen. I've already been in line for half an hour."

"Fine," said Julie with a disappointed grin. She turned toward Teresa. "Would you box up five dozen for this gentleman?"

"Five dozen, coming up," replied Teresa.

An elderly lady was next in line.

Julie renewed her smile. "How may I help you, ma'am?"

"I'd like six dozen sugar cookies, please," replied the lady.

Julie's smile faded a bit again. "Oh boy. Okay, ma'am, how many would you need just to tide you over a couple days?"

✳ ✳ ✳

The Christmas cookie hoarders would not be denied. The Shellys kept trying to cajole customers and stretch their limited supply, but gave up after barely an hour, as the cookies dwindled far faster than the crowd and it became evident many customers would leave empty-handed. The Shellys made 250 dozen cookies in preparation for opening night, only 25 dozen more than opening night the previous year. But it was still a serious miscalculation. All Christmas cookies sold out in under ninety minutes, with nearly $3,750 raised for the Lighthouse Adoption Network. Julie's only regret was that they did not anticipate the frenzied sales, so that they could have made even more money for Lighthouse.

Still, Julie cherished the special night. She found comfort in being an intimate part of something her grandparents and parents labored to build over the decades. She loved seeing their effort bear fruit in the community through the simple joy and pleasure that the lights and the café continued to foster. Despite the noise and chaos of the evening's work, there was a particular sweetness to those hours spent shoulder to shoulder with her family, especially because her dad was still with them. She had taken for granted his health, his unrivaled work ethic, and his rock-solid presence as the family patriarch. It dawned on her in the days since his heart attack that Perry would not always be there—something she had been lightly conscious of, but always suppressed the thought. She vowed to cherish anew each day she had with her parents. There was a none too subtle part of Julie that wondered if fulfilling her dream of traveling the world would really be worth missing out on nights like this one.

✳ ✳ ✳

Once the family finished cleaning and preparing the café for the next morning, Bev, Perry, and Teresa dropped Bonnie off at her house before returning home. Julie declined to ride with them, even though she had left her own car at home. She wanted to walk the quiet streets, feel the cold snap of the wind against her cheeks still flush from the night's exertions, and revel in the splendor of the Christmas lights.

As she neared home, her phone rang. As soon as Julie answered it, Beth chortled, "I think the movie's back."

"Fantastic. What is it now?" asked Julie, feigning annoyance.

Julie was amused by the rustling sounds of Beth multi-tasking as she talked. The shuffling of mail, plunking silverware in the dishwasher, then pouring a beverage in a glass. "You just had your own version of that part where everyone crashes the Building and Loan!"

"I totally forgot about that!"

Julie regaled Beth with details of the frantic night at Shelly's, the "run on the bakery," and the sold-out Christmas cookies. By the time Julie reached home, her curiosity was piqued anew about the crossover in recent weeks between her life and that of the fictional George Bailey. Before hanging up, she asked Beth if she thought Nosker's Video Vault (the sole remaining physical movie rental establishment in the county) would have a copy of *It's a Wonderful Life*. Beth was sure of it and even more sure that Julie should go to the trouble of procuring a copy.

Julie felt rather wide awake and wired from the evening's activity. So, upon reaching her driveway, she got in her car and drove the couple of miles across town to Nosker's Video Vault. Closing time was apparently 10:00 p.m. It was 9:58 by her watch, but the door was already locked. She knocked on the glass, hoping a friendly smile and wave would persuade the store's sole clerk to admit one last customer. The clerk, a thin, bearded, twenty-something man wearing a wool beanie, did not appear persuaded by her perky charm. He stoically trudged to the door anyway, however, and let her in.

As Beth predicted, the store did have one DVD copy of *Wonderful Life*, which the clerk found on a shelf for her without altering his level of enthusiasm in the slightest.

"Have you ever seen this?" asked Julie, trying to pierce the gloomy fluorescent atmosphere with some humanity.

"Nope," muttered the clerk.

"It's really great. I'm not much of an old movie person, but I highly recommend it."

"Cool," he replied, clearly not finding anything cool about her movie review.

Julie gladly paid the three-dollar rental fee with a five-dollar bill, letting the clerk keep the change for his trouble, though her gesture still did not move the needle on his mirth.

Julie returned home, changed into her favorite pajamas, and began watching the movie with renewed intrigue, her eyes peeled for new details and clues. Twenty-five minutes into the movie, however, exhaustion finally caught up with her and she drifted asleep on her couch. As she did so, the DVD player remote slipped from her loosened grip to the carpeted floor. Julie slept hard as the movie continued playing on her small, flat screen television.

An hour later, veering into deep sleep, Julie had a vivid dream in which she was suddenly and inexplicably standing on the Cedar Springs steel truss bridge at night. She stood in the middle of the road, alone, squinting as she gazed across the bridge, though she did not know what she was searching for. In her dream, the bridge's Christmas lights suddenly began flashing on and off, slowly at first, then at an increasing rate that echoed her own heart beating faster and faster. An icy wind roared just before a blizzard erupted, with heavy, blinding snow blowing into her face from across the bridge. She buried her eyes and nose in the sleeve of her right elbow for protection. In that instant, with the bridge lights still pulsating all around her, the headlights of a car bore down on her. The car was moving fast and at the last possible second, she dove to her right to avoid being struck...

Julie jolted awake, her dream disrupted by the sudden on-screen yelling. She sat up, disoriented, and rubbed her eyes, slowly refocusing on the television. Onscreen, George Bailey was desperately confronting his Uncle Billy, trying to get him to remember what happened to a missing $8,000 Building and Loan deposit. She continued watching a while longer, though she was preoccupied with her strange dream. It was more of a nightmare really. It had seemed so real. She tried to distract herself with the movie, in which George and Clarence, the angel, were ordering drinks at a bar. But as George and Clarence conversed, Julie's eyelids once again grew too heavy to lift. She found the remote on the floor, clicked off the television, shuffled the few feet to her bedroom, and collapsed in bed.

Chapter 17

When her radio alarm sounded the following morning, Julie found it difficult to eject herself from bed. She regretted her decision to stay up late watching the movie, as she had not actually finished it and seemingly gained no additional insights into her own situation from the little she viewed. She also lost valuable sleep that could have helped curb her foggy fatigue that lingered even after being at work for an hour.

Around 9:45 that morning, Julie was going through the motions behind the counter, yawning frequently, wondering if she would have time to squeeze in a power nap during her lunch break. She gave a male customer his change at the cash register and, as the man walked toward the exit, she casually glanced out the café's front windows. She glimpsed a man peering through the glass into the café as if he was looking for someone. Julie was about to head to the kitchen but took a second glance at the stranger looking through the window. Then she briefly scanned the café to see who the man might be looking for. None of the other customers indicated any sign of interest in the man at the window.

The man peering inside the café had silver hair and looked to be about Perry's age. He was dressed a bit like a man on a hunting trip by way of a Norman Rockwell painting—dark blue jeans over laced up work boots, a green flannel plaid shirt under a wool-lined denim coat, and a red plaid hunting cap with the flaps that covered his ears. Julie's curiosity was tied to the man's persistent smile as he peered through the window, as if something amused him.

Julie began wiping down a counter that didn't really need it, while she kept a subtle eye on the man as he entered the café. He stood briefly in the entryway, still smiling as he took in the environs. Seemingly satisfied, he turned his attention to the card rack near the cash register, stepped over to it, and began perusing the cards. He carefully examined several cards but only picked up one—the one with the cover photograph of the Cedar Springs bridge adorned with white Christmas lights. He grinned, apparently content with his selection. He pulled the accompanying envelope from the rack behind the small stack of cards. Then he stepped up to the counter and waited patiently, the card and envelope in his right hand.

Julie quickly tossed her towel under the counter and smiled at the man.

"Hi!" she said. "All set?"

"Pardon?"

"Are you ready to check out?"

"Yes, ma'am," he replied, smiling warmly and setting the card on the counter.

Julie immediately noted the bridge-photo card. Without thinking, her smile dimmed slightly, and she glanced at the man with more surprise in her eyes than she would have preferred to convey in an ideal reaction. The odd dream flashed through her mind—her standing on the bridge, the flashing lights, almost getting run over by a car. She quickly caught herself and picked up the card to scan the barcode. "Can I get you a coffee or anything to go?"

Her question seemed to fluster the man for a moment as he considered the option. "Hmm, well, I suppose. Maybe." He studied the menu boards.

"Is this your first visit to Shelly's?"

A brief, blank expression enveloped the man's face. In his hesitance, Julie was not sure he understood her question, or thought perhaps he had difficulty hearing, so she clarified. "Have you been in to see us before?"

"Why no, actually. This is my first time. You have a very lovely establishment."

"Thank you. We appreciate that. Well, since it's your first visit, your coffee is on the house."

"Oh. Well, that's very kind."

Julie turned to get a medium to-go cup. "That's the way we get repeat customers, see, we get 'em hooked on our coffee." She smiled at the man who seemed slightly slow on the uptake, but he finally chuckled. "So, what kind would you like? Right now we have a dark roast, a hazelnut, French roast, and our medium house blend."

"Oh my. Well, I don't guess I know. What would you recommend?"

"Well, they're all very good, but hazelnut is probably my current favorite."

"I'm sure it will be my favorite too then."

"Hazelnut it is!" Julie filled the cup with coffee from the hazelnut urn, then snapped on a disposable plastic lid, and handed it to the man. "And if you'd like any cream or sugar, it's right over there." She pointed to her right, toward the coffee condiments station on the other side of the pastry case.

"Thank you very much. I'm sure this will be terrific on its own." He held the cup of coffee gingerly, with two hands, as if holding radioactive material. He made a slight turn toward the exit, then remembered his card on the counter and turned back.

"Okay sir, your total for the card is $3.75."

He set his coffee on the counter beside the card and pulled a worn leather wallet from his front right jeans pocket. Julie noticed his wallet seemed exceptionally thin. There did not appear to be anything in the wallet except two bills, which he removed and handed to Julie with another smile. She returned his smile and glanced at the bills—both were two-dollar bills.

"We don't get many two-dollar bills," she said, as she put the currency in the cash register and pulled out a quarter in change. "Twenty-five cents is your change…" she held out the quarter, but the man had already picked up his card and was halfway to the café door. "Sir," she called out, "your change!"

She ripped the receipt from the register and stepped around the counter after the man, who exited the café. Rather impulsively for Julie, she rushed out of the café, still wearing her SB&C apron. She saw the man continuing down the sidewalk and tried calling out again, "Sir, you forgot your change!"

Ordinarily, she would have given up on such a pursuit. However, there was something peculiar about the man—the way she first glimpsed him peering curiously through the front window and his only purchase being the Christmas card with the bridge photo. But it was his hesitance ordering coffee that tripped something oddly familiar in her mind, and as she made her way out of the café and onto the front sidewalk, she suddenly realized what it was. She would not want to admit it to anyone (with the possible exception of Beth) because it sounded bonkers, but the man's hesitance reminded her of the last scene she watched from *It's a Wonderful Life* the previous night before falling asleep: Clarence, ordering a drink at the bar. She mostly dismissed the thought as pathetic wishful thinking. She was probably just connecting the dots because the scene was fresh on her mind, having percolated in her subconscious overnight. Nevertheless, propelledby impatient curiosity, she continued her light pursuit of the man down the sidewalk.

The man in the plaid hunting cap suddenly sensed Julie following him and quickened his steps.

Julie was surprised by her own atypical assertiveness and bravery. "Excuse me, sir?" she called out. The man seemed to speed up his walk some more and Julie was pretty sure she saw him steal a glance over his shoulder. "Sir! Wait, please!" she tried again, louder.

The stranger started jogging. This unforeseen escalation astounded Julie. He was apparently much spryer than he initially appeared. It also fueled her hunch that there was more to him than met the eye. She jogged after him. She might not quite match the fitness level of her parents at their finest, nor her brother Hugh, but she was at least a twice-weekly jogger and confident she could catch an old man running with a cup of coffee.

Her confidence was misplaced. The old man was shockingly swift.

The man made a sharp left turn off the sidewalk into the middle of Main Street. A fortuitous break in traffic allowed him to speed walk across the street to the small city park. Julie reached the spot where the man cut across Main Street, but the traffic resumed its flow and she had to wait for several passing cars. Finally, Julie had an opening to continue her jog across the street and into the park, but the traffic pause put some distance between her and the stranger.

To Julie's left up ahead, she saw a police cruiser descending the inclined street that ran parallel to the sloped city park. She had a hunch it was Beth but sincerely hoped it wasn't, since it would be rather difficult to explain (even to her best friend) the peculiar sight of her chasing down an elderly man jogging with his cup of coffee. As soon as the police cruiser whipped left into the nearest parking space adjacent to the park grounds, her fear was confirmed. Beth opened her car door just as the man jogged past her.

"Officer! There's a woman chasing me!" shouted the man. He half-turned to point at Julie who was slightly gaining on him.

Beth followed the man's gesture. "You don't say..." she said with a wry smile.

The man slowed his jog to a brisk walk, continuing through the heart of the park. Beth turned back to address him, but he was already a considerable distance away. She barely had time to marvel at his speed before Julie arrived and put her hands on her hips, trying to catch her breath. "Why'd you let him get away?" she sputtered.

"I didn't realize we had a criminal on our hands. What's wrong?"

"He forgot his change! And his receipt." She held up the receipt for emphasis.

"Whoa. I better put out an APB then."

"There was something really odd about him. At first he was just looking in the window."

"So? Maybe the guy wanted a muffin. Why the heck were you chasing him? You probably scared the poor dude to death! That's not great for customer loyalty."

"It wasn't just that. He finally came in, and only bought one thing." Julie paused, slowly shaking her head in wonder.

"What'd he buy?" asked Beth impatiently.

"That Christmas card. The one with the bridge covered in lights on the front."

"The same one you got in the mail from 1986?"

"Yep!"

"Dang. So maybe we found our prankster. Maybe he's about to go put another card hit on somebody."

Julie shrugged. "Oh, and this is the other weird part—he paid with a couple of two-dollar bills. Who does that?"

"Only the most hardened criminals," deadpanned Beth. "That's their calling card—paying with two-dollar bills."

"Really?"

"No!"

"And there was one other thing."

"What?"

"He didn't know what coffee to order. Kinda reminded me of Clarence in the movie."

"Right, right—when he orders a drink at the bar!" Beth wore an amused expression, but it was tinged with concern she may have unduly contributed to the demise of her best friend's sanity.

"Weird, right?" asked Julie, fishing for assurance.

"I mean, not as weird as you chasing him through the park, but...look, we might be taking this whole thing a bit far, don't you think? You might've traumatized that poor guy."

Julie did not believe in elaborate conspiracies or aliens, so if any of this added up to the universe trying to tell her something, as far as she was concerned, it must be God-initiated. She was familiar enough with the Bible to recall several instances when angels interacted with humans. She could not fathom why her life might merit any visit by a special messenger from the Lord. But in the off chance that was one of them buying a Christmas card earlier, she desperately craved confirmation. While rehashing the episode with Beth, it also dawned on Julie that God's messengers in the Bible did not typically run away from their message recipients. So, it was quite possible she was actually full-blown nuts.

Just then, Julie heard the bell of the courthouse clock strike 10:00 a.m. and it triggered another alarming thought. "Wait a minute—Aunt Bonnie! I gotta go!" She suddenly bolted away from Beth, back down the park's paved path toward Main Street.

"What's wrong now?" called Beth.

"No time!" was the only explanation Julie left flapping in the air.

Julie ran straight for the nearest crosswalk this time, since she was a general law abider and did not want to put Beth in the awkward position of having to give her a jaywalking citation. As soon as Julie reached the opposite sidewalk, she resumed jogging all the way back to the café entrance where her mom stood outside wearing a quizzical look.

"What's going on?" Bev asked with equal parts amusement and concern.

"Did Bonnie already leave for the bank?"

"I think so. Why?"

"I'll explain later!" Julie ran up the sidewalk, this time in the opposite direction from which she had chased the man a few moments earlier.

Bev called after her, "Are you okay?"

Chapter 18

Julie had always been fairly logical, careful, and methodical in her approach to decision-making and life in general. In grade school she was typically one of the last students to finish any sort of test, as she always checked and re-checked her answers before turning it in. She was not quite obsessive-compulsive in her behavior, although her family occasionally teased her to that effect.

Perry and Bev were blessed with common sense, which they endowed to Julie and Hugh. Julie knew chasing the older gentleman through the park was neither methodical nor an application of common sense. It was instead a rare moment of impulse for her, a giant leap outside her usual modus operandi. It was acting on instinct—something she had often heard from and read about in others, but was usually insecure about trying herself (mainly because of her spotty *acting-on-instinct* record in adolescence). She startled herself with the split-second decision to run after the stranger. Yet, particularly after his purchase of the bridge-photo Christmas card, along with her bizarre dream, she felt an eerie, instant coalescence of all the *It's a Wonderful Life* coincidences that preceded it. Coupled with the movie's prominence in her mind from her partial viewing the night before, she felt the unusual urge that she *must* try to talk to the man. She was also aware that, mostly, she just craved answers to the questions piling up.

Now, even though she seemingly barked up the wrong tree in running after the man in the hunting cap, her heightened intuition stubbornly convinced her these coincidences had a purpose. She reasoned part of that purpose might include the fact Aunt Bonnie had already departed for the Cedar Springs State Bank intending to deposit all of the previous night's SB&C cash. The bulk of that money was the Christmas cookie profit earmarked for the Lighthouse Adoption Network. Surely it was no mere coincidence Julie awoke the previous night precisely at the part of the movie where George is at wit's end with Uncle Billy, trying to discover what happened to their $8,000 Building and Loan deposit. Julie could not yet solve the puzzle; she just *knew* she must get to the bank in time to ensure no mishap occurred with Bonnie and the café's charitable deposit. For all she knew, Bonnie might have already fumbled the cash into a street gutter by now.

Still wearing her SB&C apron, Julie completed her madcap jaunt down the sidewalk along Main Street, dodging pedestrians and dog-walkers, past the courthouse, and then another two blocks to Cedar Springs State Bank. She leapt up the bank's front entrance steps and thrust open the heavy front door. In hastily barreling through the door however, she bowled over none other than Harriet Paddock.

Harriet's left forearm took the brunt of the blow, but the force of Julie's desperate entrance sent Harriet stumbling backwards. Knocked entirely off balance, she tripped on her own feet and tumbled onto her right hip. Harriet's cane slid across the polished tile floor, and the whole world seemed to pause, holding its breath in anxious silence. She laid back and groaned, her head resting on the floor. She was dazed and slowly writhed with abandon.

Julie immediately clasped her hands over her mouth in utter shock and horror, her wide-eyed stare fixed on the crumpled Harriet.

"Oh, my back! My hip! Ohhhhhh…my neck!" Harriet could not settle on a precise ailment. Her whole body was wracked in pain, or so she projected to the growing number of gawkers. The whole bank ground to a halt as everyone stared at Harriet sprawled on the floor.

"Oh, my gosh, Harriet!" Julie stooped to Harriet's side to offer assistance. "I am so sorry!" She delicately placed a hand on Harriet's left arm, but Harriet huffily brushed away Julie's gesture.

"I bet you are. Don't touch me, moron, you'll jostle my spine. I may be paralyzed. Someone call 911!"

Julie remained kneeling beside Harriet, but she was frozen. Bonnie, who missed the collision while conversing with a bank teller, finally tuned in to what everyone was staring at and rushed over to the scene.

"What the heck happened?" asked Bonnie with astonishment.

"Your idiot niece happened, that's what! No doubt trying to finish me off to delay the trial!"

"Harriet, believe me, it was a complete accident! I feel terrible!"

"Not as terrible as you're going to feel. My lawyer's going to have a field day with this!"

"I thought *you* were your lawyer," remarked Bonnie, rather dryly. Julie almost managed a smirk at what she knew was unintentional pithiness from her aunt.

Harriet ignored Bonnie's statement and groaned some more. "Oh, my head! Has anyone called 911 yet?"

The female bank manager and another male staffer joined the accident scene to check on Harriet. Julie finally stood and Bonnie leaned in closer, asking, "*You* ran over her? What on earth were you in such a rush for?"

Julie could not look Bonnie in the eye. Her cheeks flushed as a wave of intense embarrassment and concern overtook her. "Uh…it's kind of hard to explain. Did you make the deposit?"

"Of course!" Bonnie held up the deposit slip in one hand and her smartphone in the other. A reminder tone sounded from her phone, and Bonnie checked the accompanying message on the screen. "Oh, yes. I'm supposed to stop by the pharmacy next. Thank goodness for these reminders, huh?"

"Right," was all Julie managed in reply as she brought her left hand to her forehead in distress. She looked down at Harriet who was still grimacing theatrically on the floor. Julie's ears felt hot. She could not remember the last time she felt like she was in such trouble. Worst-case scenarios flashed through her mind: Harriet suing, Julie's travel savings evaporating toward legal fees, the SB&C shutting down. Or perhaps even Julie going to prison.

Harriet lay on the floor for a few minutes until the female bank manager finally convinced her to sit up, and then, with evolutionary slowness, helped her to stand. Julie lingered on the fringes of the scene, knowing there was nothing further she could say to make Harriet believe the accident was anything other than an assassination attempt. The bank staffers helped Harriet to a chair in the waiting area of the lobby. Harriet loudly insisted on calling an ambulance.

Once Julie saw the ambulance approaching outside the bank windows, she knew there was no reason to hang around, so she trudged back to Shelly's, loaded down with bewilderment and dread.

✳ ✳ ✳

By the time Julie arrived at the café, Bonnie had already apprised the family with details of Julie's bank showdown with Harriet. There was plenty of concern, as well as stifled chuckles from cousin Teresa. None of them could fathom the odds Julie would run over Harriet like that, with all the baggage it entailed. The family was curious why Julie rushed to the bank in the first place. Julie was in no mood to explain. They tried to reassure her that, like most of Harriet's antics, this would amount to nothing. But Julie did *not* share their confidence.

Julie finished her shift in relative silence as a thick cloud of melancholy and anxiety enveloped her. When they were children, Hugh sometimes referred to this cloud as the "Julie Gloom," until she finally punched him in the nose for saying it in one of her rare, ill-fated, impulsive moments. From then on, he mostly said it behind her back. Julie was no longer as prone to these gloomy bouts, but when they occasionally hit, they struck hard, and there was little anyone could do to pull her out of the depressive vortex.

✳ ✳ ✳

That night, alone in her apartment over the garage, Julie sifted through the complex emotions plaguing her. She was humiliated by the Harriet incident, and even more so by the reason that spurred her sprint to the bank. She wondered if this was what a slow descent into madness felt like. She thought about doing an Internet search for "early warning signs of insanity" but decided against it, since it would probably just make her further paranoid and depressed. She tried to suppress the thought as she usually did when it periodically surfaced—*she wasn't depressed. What did she possibly have to be depressed about? A wonderful, loving family. Dear friends. A stable job in the family business. Money in the bank she'd been saving for years for a trip now just over two weeks away. Her cup overflowed. So why this ongoing battle with feeling dissatisfied, wanting to leave Cedar Springs, wanting to follow her own course and agenda? Was that a form of depression?*

Julie went round and round with herself. Finally, she decided to try to quiet the thoughts with chores, so she began tidying her living space. She shelved several travel books strewn about the room. She put used mugs, bowls, and spoons in the small dishwasher. She folded clean clothes that were wrinkled from spending a week in the laundry basket on her couch. Then she spotted the *It's a Wonderful Life* DVD case lying open beside the television. She picked up the remote and ejected the disc from the DVD player. She started to snap the disc into the case but caught herself. Those nagging thoughts returned...the coincidences...that dream in which she was almost roadkill...the odd Christmas card and what, if any, connection it had to the peculiar customer at Shelly's that morning.

Of course, she was also totally wrong about Bonnie and the bank deposit.

She sighed in frustration at herself and finally decided to give the movie one last shot. She popped the disc back into the player and clicked on the television. She sank into her couch and grabbed a pen and one of the numerous *Moleskine* notebooks that littered her apartment. She skipped ahead in the movie, not sure where to resume her search since she did not even know what she was looking for. Finally, she landed on an unnerving scene in which George Bailey discovers the headstone of his brother, Harry. The angel, Clarence, explains to George that in this alternate version of his life, Harry died as a child because George was not there to save him from drowning in the frozen pond. George is distraught.

Julie leaned forward, absorbed in the drama...until a sudden, loud knock on her door startled her and she fumbled the remote control. She quickly recovered, reluctantly paused the movie, and sprang off the couch to answer the door. She opened it to find her parents, Beth, and Eric all standing on the stairs.

"Uh, did I miss a caroling memo or something?" she wondered, stepping aside to allow everyone in from the cold.

There was little reaction to Julie's attempt at humor. Julie did not care for the awkward vibe from the miniature mob.

Finally, in the specific, caring tone Julie had heard all her life, Bev said, "Honey, we're just a little worried about you."

"Okay." Julie squinted suspiciously. "Why's that?"

"I told them everything," blurted Beth, cringing as she spoke.

"Told them what?"

"You know. About you thinking your life is turning into George Bailey's."

Julie scoffed. "Well, I've never said *that* exactly."

Julie's protest was severely undermined by the paused close-up of George Bailey maniacally gripping Clarence's coat collar, which filled the television screen directly behind her. The image was impossible to ignore, and the group exchanged bemused glances. Julie glanced over her shoulder at the screen, then hastily located her remote and clicked off the television in a futile attempt to blunt the evidence.

"Besides," continued Julie, "you're the one who kept pointing out all this stuff. I thought you believed it too. A lot of times more than *I* did."

"But you chased an old man down the street and then took out an old lady," said Beth as empathetically as she could.

"Okay, Harriet was a complete accident. And in my defense, that old guy was acting pretty suspicious. Right?" Julie hoped for some backup from Beth, though none materialized.

"We know you've been under a ton of stress lately with Dad's heart attack, and running the café, and your trip coming up..." Bev said.

"Sweetie, maybe you should talk with Pastor Tim," offered Perry in his steady, compassionate tone.

"I do *not* need to talk to the pastor about this, Dad."

"Honey, we're just worried about you," said Perry, "So if you need to talk..."

Julie put her head in her hands. "This is seriously embarrassing. And unbelievable. Thanks, Beth."

"Please don't blame Beth," said Bev. "I called her because I was worried about you today. And I roped her into coming over here."

Julie's tone turned emphatic. "Listen, I appreciate everyone's concern, but I'm absolutely fine. One hundred percent sane. Really. I don't need any counseling or shrink sessions. Everything's under control. You're just going to have to trust me."

Bev stepped over and put her arm around Julie. "We trust you, dear. Can we just hear you say it though?"

"Say *what*?" asked Julie, thoroughly irritated.

"That you don't think you're George Bailey."

"Mom!" Julie looked incredulously at Beth again. "I really wish you hadn't worded it that way."

Beth winced back at her friend, apologizing with her eyes.

"Well," continued Bev, "it's just that, you know, didn't he want to commit suicide in the movie?"

"When have I ever struck y'all as being remotely suicidal? That's it, everyone out." Julie stepped over to the door and opened it. "I need to get started on the long hibernation it's going to take for me to shake off this humiliation, so…Merry Christmas and to all a good night."

Everyone slowly filed out. Bev and Perry gave Julie quick hugs on their way. Beth mouthed, "*I'm sorry!*" to Julie, whose only reply was a slight grimace.

Ordinarily, Julie liked to stay up late at night. She knew she was perpetually sleep deprived, but she could not help herself, as there was always an article or book to read, something to add to her journal, photos to edit, an aspect of her travel plans to work on. Those precious late-night hours were her escape; time she used to stoke her dreams. But that night, she was depleted. As soon as she chased everyone out the door, she trudged to her bedroom and fell face down on the bed, mortified and frustrated. Eventually, she turned over onto her back, and pulled the comforter over her.

She stared at the ceiling, replaying the day in her mind. She wished she had done better explaining to her family how much she *knew* it was ludicrous to think her life had any sort of connection to a seventy-plus-year-old movie. Yet, she also wished she could remind them how uncanny so many of the events of the past few weeks had been. She wondered if they already forgot about the strange Christmas card with the 1986 postmark. If nothing else, that one was peculiar. *That* got her attention.

She longed to be understood, but she knew no one could fully comprehend how she felt about the coincidences. Though she was full of skepticism, she could not shirk the growing feeling that these coincidences *did* mean something; that they *did* have something to do with her life. That God *was* trying to tell her something important, or that she was being spurred to do something. She felt rather childish for thinking those things, yet she had never experienced anything remotely like this. And *that* was difficult to ignore.

Of course, she also returned to the possibility she was slowly losing her mind. Perhaps she needed to discuss the matter with Pastor Tim after all.

Her thoughts drifted to Van. He was the only person who knew about the *Wonderful Life* connections and had not doubted her sanity—at least not openly. She considered calling him but could not get past the awkward memory of their most recent interactions. She shuddered anew at the thought of making him feel rejected that night at the café. She wondered what if, instead, she had said she loved him back? And what if she had said it because it might be true? It occurred to her that all her relationships were vibrant and healthy before she watched that dumb movie and allowed it to take up residence in her head. Exhausted and weary of her mental merry-go-round, she whispered aloud a prayer. If any of this was God communicating something to her, would He please make it clear, and obvious? Because in her own opinion, she was generally blind, deaf, and dumb in spiritual matters. She would not even object to some handwriting on the wall, freaky though that would be.

She clicked off the bedside lamp and closed her eyes, but sleep came far too slowly as she remembered Harriet and the impending trial.

Chapter 19

Following what Harriet Paddock deemed Julie's "attack" on her inside the bank, Harriet finagled an emergency court hearing to request an injunction on the Shellys' lights display. So, on the Tuesday following Friday's lamentable bank incident, Perry and Mike were back in the courtroom, seated at the defense table. Julie once again sat in the gallery, where she was surprised to find at least a dozen other townsfolk apparently there to witness any potential drama firsthand. She could not help but roll her eyes when Harriet entered the courtroom in a wheelchair, pushed up the center aisle by the bailiff. Harriet glared at Julie as she rolled by and Julie did her best to maintain a calm visage that belied her anxiety.

Julie grew impatient waiting for the proceeding to begin. She questioned her decision to be there because her nervousness worsened with each excruciating minute. She thought perhaps it would have been better to be nervous at work where at least she had plenty of tasks to help distract her. But she opted to attend the hearing so that the nerve-wracking suspense would subside as early as possible.

Julie was pleased to see Harriet was still representing herself. No one understood why she did so. After all, if anyone in Cedar Springs could afford a fancy lawyer it was surely Harriet. However, as long as Harriet flew solo on this, Julie was more confident Harriet would be tripped up along the way and squander any case that an actual lawyer might mount.

Judge Goodrich finally arrived, took her seat, and commenced the hearing. Harriet had the floor first and she relished her big moment, struggling to maneuver her wheelchair out from behind the plaintiff table and around in front of the judge's bench. Harriet wore braces on both knees and both elbows. Julie's amusement at Harriet's theatrics quickly faded when Harriet produced surveillance video from the bank clearly depicting Julie as she burst through the front doors and plowed into Harriet. Harriet played the video clip on a loop for maximum effect.

Julie studied Judge Goodrich's face. The judge seemed intrigued by Harriet's presentation, which only deepened Julie's anxiety.

"Your Honor, it is my sincere belief that this video is compelling evidence that a close member of Perry Shelly's family deliberately attempted to inflict injury on my person. It was a blatant effort to compromise this case and try to ensure the family's public nuisance of a Christmas lights show keeps right on going." Harriet looked quite pleased with her opening barrage.

Julie figured Harriet probably spent considerable time rehearsing that spiel. Harriet aroused unholy feelings in Julie that she hardly knew she was capable of.

"Furthermore, because of this terrifying development, I would like to request an injunction to immediately shut down the Shelly lights display. Because it seems inappropriate for Mr. Shelly to continue profiting from the display when his own daughter has clearly attempted to harass and intimidate me by an assault made to look like an accident."

Julie genuinely felt terrible for knocking over Harriet at the bank. But she ached to defend herself against the injustice of Harriet spinning the complete accident into an intentional assault. She resisted the urge to sprint over and dump Harriet out of the wheelchair she likely did not even need.

Once Judge Goodrich confirmed Harriet was finished with her presentation, and after Harriet finally rolled herself back behind the plaintiff's table, Mike rose to speak.

"Your honor," Mike began coolly, "First, I would like to correct Ms. Paddock regarding my client's profiting from the lights display. Unlike many similar displays around the country, the Shelly family has never charged admission. Not once in seventy years. Ultimately, this is a simple matter. The plaintiff's recent accident, while unfortunate, is quite obviously, as evident in the surveillance video, just that—an accident. However, the plaintiff's accident, and this video 'evidence' has no bearing on this suit anyway. My client had nothing to do with the plaintiff's accident. The plaintiff is trying to garner the court's sympathy and circumvent the actual trial because she knows her case is weak. My client is accused of running a Christmas lights display that is a 'public nuisance.' We have overwhelming testimony available to contradict that false notion. The Shelly Family Christmas Lights Spectacular has been a community treasure and a beloved Christmas time tradition for decades. Ms. Paddock is apparently attempting to make these frivolous lawsuits an annual Christmas tradition of her own. I hope the court will see this for what it is—a quibble from one individual about Christmas lights that a vast majority of Cedar Springs citizens, as well as those from surrounding communities, do *not* want to see shut down."

Mike returned to his seat beside Perry, who gave him an appreciative nod. Julie wanted to applaud but restrained herself. She thought surely Harriet did not stand a chance against Mike's eloquence.

Unlike previous county judge Ed Rogers, who retired nine months earlier, Judge Goodrich was new to the bench, unfamiliar with Harriet's lawsuit attempts from past Christmases, and thus unpredictable. Judge Goodrich sat in pensive silence for a couple of minutes, occasionally jotting some notes. Julie could hardly bear the suspense, wondering what the judge could possibly be pondering. To Julie, this was a clear-cut case of a bitter old woman working overtime to be the town Scrooge.

Finally, Judge Goodrich straightened her posture and addressed Harriet, Perry, and Mike. "Ms. Paddock, you've presented me with a dilemma. On one hand, your argument is barking up the wrong legal tree. After all, Mr. Shelly's daughter is not technically a party in this lawsuit. On the other hand, this new video evidence is impossible to ignore and may have some relevance in this case. It bears further investigation."

Julie felt suddenly sick with fear Harriet might go after her next and try to get Julie charged with assault or something.

"And Mr. Hughes, while it is possible that Ms. Paddock's opinion that the Shelly Family's Christmas lights display may be, as you indicated, a 'minority' opinion, it does not mean that the display is *not* a public nuisance, as she asserts."

Julie could not see the faces of her dad and Mike to discern their reactions to the judge's words, but it seemed to Julie the judge was about to deliver bad news.

"In light of the new developments in this case, the trial will be rescheduled for January eighth."

Mike stood in protest, "Your honor, with all due respect..." Judge Goodrich held up her hand to halt his words.

"And furthermore," continued the judge, "because of the new development in this case, I am granting a temporary injunction to shut down the lights display beginning today, until the trial is over."

"But your honor, dozens of volunteers worked for over two weeks in coordination with the city to put up these lights. Surely you wouldn't have their efforts squandered. The lights would be taken down around the same time as the start of the trial anyway. I would ask that you reconsider and leave them on at least through Christmas," said Mike.

"I'm not sure what you're accustomed to Mr. Hughes, but in my courtroom, protests after I've issued a decision are entirely out of bounds."

Judge Goodrich smacked her gavel, and swiftly turned to leave the courtroom. Mike looked at Perry, rather stunned. Julie's heart sank. She wondered if she correctly understood the judge about the lights being turned off immediately.

✳ ✳ ✳

Julie waited in the hallway outside the courtroom for Perry and Mike. She hugged Perry when he finally emerged. "I'm so sorry, Dad."

"Everything will be okay," Perry replied, with a bit less certainty in his eyes than usual when trying to reassure Julie about something.

Mike exited the courtroom a moment later, rushing past them and out the main courthouse doors.

"Mike!" Julie jogged after him outside. "Mike, wait!"

Mike finally paused and turned to face her on the courthouse steps. The sky was heavily overcast, and snow flurries swirled around them.

"I'm kind of on a tight schedule today, so…"

His remark stung Julie. "Okay. Well, I won't keep you. I just thought, I don't know…. Harriet doesn't really have a shot here, does she?"

"I don't know, Julie. She might now. Your little bank stunt sure doesn't help."

Julie felt even further stung, having never heard Mike sound so sharp and abrupt. "I'm *really* sorry. If I could just explain what happened…"

He cut her off with, "No need. Your dad told me everything." She winced. "All the stuff about the movie, and…"

"Yeah." He paused, glancing at the ground for a moment while carefully choosing his words. He finally looked Julie in the eyes. "I would keep a very tight lid on all that if I were you."

"So, you think I'm crazy too?"

"Come on, Julie, it's absurd. I mean, if Harriet gets wind of that, you'll never hang a Christmas light in this county again. I don't think you're crazy, but, you know, maybe you should talk to someone or something. Okay? I've got to go."

"Sorry for wasting your time," was all the response she could manage as she fought back tears.

Mike turned and rushed down the steps, leaving Julie feeling very alone and exposed in the icy wind. She returned inside the courthouse to find her dad. She admired his positive effort in these circumstances, though she wondered how he could muster even a fake smile at this point.

On the short car ride back to the SB&C, Perry explained his smile was genuine. "When you come within a whisker of death and God decides to spare you awhile longer, there's not much worth getting down about. So downtown's going to be a little less bright this year. But she can't cancel Christmas."

Julie finally smiled too, thankful her dad was able to snap things back into perspective like that. She felt foolish for failing to maintain that perspective on her own in the days since his heart attack. She felt the brief flutter of butterflies in her stomach, thinking about leaving her parents soon to travel the world. She wondered if she could really leave them for that long, these two saints who had given her everything.

That night, for the first time in seventy years, the Shelly Family Christmas Lights Spectacular was extinguished by Judge Goodrich's court order. The remaining Christmas lights shining in Cedar Springs were now confined to neighborhoods, plus the smattering strung by the city, including the strands adorning the old, red, steel truss bridge on the eastern edge of downtown.

Chapter 20

Julie pulled into the mostly empty parking lot of the aging Cedar Springs High School stadium, where she could see Van on the field wrapping up the afternoon's soccer practice. Hurting Van's feelings weighed heavily on Julie since the last time they spoke outside Ancelloti's restaurant. With her recent humiliations, plus the previous day's courtroom setback, she wanted to reboot her life, which definitely included mending fences with Van. She missed her corny friend.

Julie entered the stadium through the open main gate and crossed the rubber track as the boys soccer team members sauntered past on their way to the locker room. She lamented not attending more of their games that season. For several years, she had served as the team's unofficial photographer, taking most of the photos Van used to put together the slide show for the annual end-of-season banquet. It dawned on her wistfully that she would not be in Cedar Springs next year to photograph games for Van.

Even from across the field, she thought Van looked to be in an extra chipper mood, which boded well for her making amends. When he noticed her approaching, he looked surprised, and Julie thought she detected a flicker of concern in his eyes, as if her arrival might have dampened his mood. She tried to ward off her paranoia.

"Hey, Coach!" began Julie, opting for the bouncy, jokey emphasis on "Coach" as her opening.

"Julie Shelly. This is rare," he replied with a grin, but in a slightly more neutral tone.

Julie made a snap decision not to delay her mission. "I need to apologize."

"What for?" he asked.

"You know. The other night after the sledding incident…"

He quickly interjected, "You mean, *Van-sledding*? Trademark pending." He smiled, but she saw through his dollop of humor and knew he was trying to diffuse the awkwardness he still felt about confessing his feelings for her that night.

"*Van-sledding*. Right. Well, I had a really good time, and…"

In his nervousness he interrupted again. "Right up until the part where I ruined everything by saying 'I love you'?"

"You didn't ruin anything. Don't beat yourself up. I mean, I'm glad you said it."

Surprise washed over his face. "You are?"

"I didn't mean to hurt you."

"I know."

"I really miss hanging out with you."

"I really miss you too."

They smiled and their eyes locked for a second longer than they were accustomed to with each other.

"And the other day when you saw me out with Mike…"

"It's okay. Really."

"No, but…"

"Julie, seriously. Forget about it."

"Please just let me explain."

"Okay. I'm sorry. Continue."

"I just want you to know I was not being hypocritical. I wasn't on some kind of date with Mike. We were leaving the courthouse; he asked me if I wanted to go get lunch. That's all."

"I know. You tried to explain the other day, but I was too interested in acting like a pouty teenager. I can be pretty good at it since I'm around them all the time. I admit—I was jealous."

"Well, don't be. Believe me, he's not too interested in anything beyond getting lunch."

"But you are?"

"I would say 'was.' And it was a very fleeting feeling, based on very poor evidence."

He grinned and teased, "Let me guess...*It's a Wonderful Life*?"

Julie shook her head at her folly. Van slung his backpack over his shoulder and they slowly began walking across the field toward the main stands.

"I seriously never should've watched that movie. You think I'm nuts, don't you?"

"Nah. Not really."

"That might mean you're nuts too."

"I've been called worse."

"I guess I just wanted it all to mean something. To add up to something life-changing or..." She paused, glanced up at the sky for a moment, and sighed. "But real life doesn't work like that. We don't get cool, mind-blowing messages that spell out our existence for us."

"We don't?" he asked in mock surprise.

"It just seems like too many coincidences not to mean *something*. I really wish I knew what it all has to do with me."

They walked a few steps in contemplative silence.

Finally, Van said, "Well, maybe, if this stuff isn't just coincidental—maybe it's not all about *you*."

His words landed with a potent thud in Julie's mind. He had not meant it as a slight against her, and she did not take it that way. She felt rather foolish and ashamed of her own self-centeredness that she had never considered the possibility these strange events, if they were indeed some kind of legitimately divine instigation, might actually be about someone other than her. Van's almost off-handed comment was anything but that to Julie. Her mind was suddenly kindled with new possibilities and also a strange sense of relief. *Perhaps he was right*, she thought. *Perhaps it had nothing to do with her at all.*

They continued walking through the short tunnel that led from the field, underneath the stands to the parking lot.

"True. Hate to say it, but I haven't really considered that," she said. "Yeah. You're absolutely right."

"For someone whose life already has a ton of meaning and purpose, you're really obsessed with finding meaning and purpose."

"What do you mean?" she asked.

"Well, you've been talking up this round-the-world trip for years, almost like your life's been on hold. As if when you finally get to leave town, you're going to figure it all out. Not that you shouldn't go. I just don't think you're going to find any more meaning overseas than you already have here. You already have a ton of purpose. Taking care of your family. Being a friend to so many. Helping refugees. I mean, you're *beloved* in this town. You know what a rare gift that is? Most people would love to have a fraction of the impact you have here. I don't blame you for wanting to travel the world. Of course you should go. But I doubt you'll find any more significance in London, Paris, or Sydney than you already have in Cedar Springs."

She was unsure how to respond to his astute assessment, so she took a page out of Van's playbook. "Gee, when you put it that way, I'm kind of a heel for leaving."

He chuckled. "Well, you're not the only heel then. I've got an interview Tuesday at Ouachita Baptist University."

They reached her car and faced each other.

"Are you serious? Wait, where's that?"

"Arkansas. It's an assistant coach position. Men's soccer. But it's a start."

She knew he had long been interested in coaching at the college level, but she had not considered it being imminent. "That's amazing, Van. I'm so glad." She hugged him. He closed his eyes, soaking in her affection. "Except, that's far away," she added as she let go of him.

"What do you care?" he teased, "You'll be off roaming the world."

"Still. I don't like the idea of you not being here when I get back."

"Well, I don't have the job yet. It's just an interview."

Julie felt quite certain he would get the job though. They talked for a few more minutes in the parking lot, with Julie updating him on the details of the judge's injunction against the lights. But she was thoroughly distracted by the thought of Van moving away.

As Julie drove back to Shelly's, her heart sagged under the weight of Van's news about his job interview in Arkansas. She was certainly happy for him, as she knew how much the opportunity meant to him. But her throat tightened, and her eyes grew misty at the prospect of no longer seeing him every day. She could not root against her friend getting the job. But assuming he did, and not knowing where her globetrotting adventures would ultimately take her, it could be a very long time before they were together again. Regardless, their friendship would not be the same. Having spent her entire life in Cedar Springs, Julie was unaccustomed to significant change, nor the departure of loved ones. And then, as if a floodgate was suddenly opened in her mind, the realization rushed in that she was in love with Van. And she had absolutely no idea what to do about it.

Later that evening, shortly before closing time, Julie left Bonnie and Teresa in charge of the café and went for a walk. It was already dark, and the air was below freezing as Julie exited Shelly's and turned left on the sidewalk. Main Street was decidedly drearier without the family's Christmas lights. The stark reminder of Harriet Paddock's legal triumph made Julie briefly bristle with anger as she walked. She was compassionate and had a rare ability to love people, but those traits hit a wall when she thought of Harriet. This realization troubled Julie and she wondered whether she was actually very loving at all. Christ's words about loving your enemies and praying for those who persecute you echoed clearly in her mind. Yet she could not fathom doing either for Harriet. Most of the people in her daily life were pleasant enough, which made being loving a relatively simple task. It was easy to *love thy neighbor* when they were not really bothering you. She knew there were plenty of hateful people in the world, but her Cedar Springs world was small, and she wondered if her capacity for love and compassion was stunted. *How does one love an enemy exactly? How could anyone love Harriet Paddock?*

Julie's intended destination was the police station, for a surprise drop-in on Beth whom she had not seen since the unfortunate intervention at Julie's apartment. When she was just two blocks from the station, however, she spotted Beth walking in her direction on the opposite sidewalk.

"Hey!" Julie called, "I was just on my way to surprise you."

"So was I!" replied Beth.

Julie paused for a couple passing cars before trotting across to Beth's side of the street. "You were on your way to surprise yourself?" she replied, with the kind of goofy humor shared by best friends.

Beth made a sarcastic, mock laughing sound. "Judging by your *lame* humor attempt, you're not mad at me anymore for turning you in to your family?"

"I wasn't really mad at you. I'm sure Mom forced it out of you."

"She totally did. And I folded like a cheap lawn chair. I am sorry though," said Beth.

"Forget it."

"If you say so."

"I do say so."

The two friends hugged, relieved to be in sync again, and sealed their reconciliation with excited plans for Julie to come over to Beth's house after she finished closing up the SB&C for the night.

※ ※ ※

When Julie arrived at Beth's later that evening, Eric was in the kitchen making hot chocolate. Julie joined Beth on the stools at the kitchen's serving bar. While they chatted, Eric stirred two cups of cocoa and slid them in front of Julie and Beth.

"Thanks, babe! You're such a wizard in the kitchen," said Beth with the teasing, sugar-coated sarcasm that was one of the hallmarks of their marriage.

"I know," Eric replied dryly. "*Kitchen Wizard's* actually gonna be the name of my new cooking show. I just signed the deal." The women had already tuned him out.

"Okay, so I've got something kind of big to tell you," said Julie.

"Oh! Me too! You first, though," replied Beth.

"That's okay. You go."

"Really?"

"Y'all are dorks," Eric impatiently interjected, before spilling the beans: "Beth found out why Harriet hates Christmas so much."

Julie's eyes widened with anticipation at Beth, who corroborated Eric's news with a slow nod. "Yes. So, I did some digging and it turns out we have some old files at the station on Harriet's family. Apparently when Harriet was eight, her mother abandoned her on Christmas Eve. Just left. Hopped a train to California or something."

Julie shook her head at the realization.

"It gets worse," warned Beth. "Just a few days later, on New Year's Eve, Harriet's dad killed himself. Went out in the woods on their property and overdosed. Can you believe that?"

Julie continued shaking her head, astonished. "And all these years we've been shoving Christmas in Harriet's face with our lights. No wonder she can't stand us."

"Hey, she could've moved away," said Eric callously.

"Babe!" scolded Beth.

"I'm just saying," remarked Eric, as he collapsed on the living room couch.

"I had no idea!" said Julie. "So, what happened with her mom?"

"She never came back for Harriet. Didn't want her. She died in the sixties, somewhere in Oregon. And that's not all."

"What?" exclaimed Julie, alarmed there could be more.

"So, when Harriet turned eighteen, she inherited her dad's fortune, right? But she got married like a year later to a much older man who apparently just married her for her money. Reverse gold-digger-type deal. He eventually worked out a divorce and got a lot of her money in the process. Oh yeah, and the divorce was finalized around Christmas time too. Another reason she probably hates the holidays."

"You think?" snorted Eric from the living room.

"Wow," said Julie, still in disbelief.

"It turns out she's not as wealthy as everyone thinks," continued Beth. "Her dad was the businessman, but she ran all his old businesses into the ground. The orchards. The old cannery. Between that and the divorce, she barely has anything left."

"Unbelievable," said Julie.

"I know. So, what were you going to tell us?"

"Oh, right. I should've gone first because mine's nothing near that big. I'm leaving on my trip a week early. The day after Christmas."

"Whoa. Really? What's the rush?"

"I've just been thinking, why wait any longer, you know? I've already got everything planned. I talked with Mom and Dad about it. They're fine. They understand. Teresa's already here working. Hugh and his fiancée will be here. I'll just be twiddling my thumbs if I wait 'til New Year's to leave."

Beth developed a slightly mischievous smirk. "What if you leave early and miss something big? You know, with…"

"Yeah," Eric added, "what about George Bailey, and Mary, and Zuzu's petals, and oh my gaaaaah…" his voice collapsed into fake hysterical crying.

"Hilarious," said Julie sarcastically.

"Good one, honey," said Beth with equal sarcasm.

"Man, I can't get over this stuff about Harriet," said Julie. "It *almost* makes me want to go give her a hug."

"Please do! I will give you one hundred dollars to go do that right now," said Eric.

"I can't get over you leaving so soon," said Beth. "I guess I've been in denial. What am I going to do without you for a year—talk to Eric? And what if you fall in love with some hunky Australian outback dude and I'm not around to disapprove and then you marry him and live in his luxury tree house and never come back?"

Julie leaned over and side-hugged Beth. "I promise I'll invite you to our lovely outback wedding."

"You better," said Beth.

"Hey, what if your life turns out to be connected to *Crocodile Dundee*?" asked Eric, grinning at his own imagination. "Now *that* would be awesome."

Julie and Beth just stared at each other and shook their heads in solidarity over Eric's prolific tomfoolery.

Chapter 21

Julie's alarm clock woke her at 4:30 a.m. with The Ronnettes' "Frosty the Snowman" on WPVS. Her body clock was so accustomed to waking up between 4:00 and 4:30 that she almost did not need an alarm anymore, but she always set one just in case. This morning proved the necessity of such redundancy, as it was a rare morning in which her mind and eyes did not immediately snap to attention. Her eyelids were heavy, and she was momentarily disoriented as to the day, time, and planet.

She lingered on her pillow trying to clear her mind-fog and in so doing, fixated on the song on the radio—primarily the lead singer's pronunciation of "Frosty" in the song. Julie tried a few imitations in her mind, trying to place the singer's accent. Finally, enough fog lifted for her to ponder just how strange early morning mind-fog-thoughts could be.

The song neared its end and Julie turned off the clock radio. She sat up in bed, remembering her morning task and recalling what day it was: "Christmas Eve *eve*," as her mom had called it for as long as Julie could remember. A tinge of excitement about Christmas coursed through Julie, a vestige of the intense thrill she felt for the holiday as a child. This time, the familiar feeling was amplified by her pending departure on her round-the-world trip, which was now set for the day after Christmas. She suddenly felt nervous about all the last-minute details she had to take care of. Thoughts of her to-do list provided an adrenaline kick forcing her out of bed, into clothes, out the door, down the steps, and into her frozen car.

A thin layer of overnight snow glazed the landscape as she drove the abandoned, pre-dawn streets to Shelly's. Upon arrival, she retrieved the box containing the previous day's un-sold muffins and croissants from the kitchen and set the box in the front passenger seat of her car. The Shellys donated their un-sold baked goods to the Cedar Springs Food Pantry four days a week, while the other two days the goods were set aside for the Congolese refugee families.

Julie drove the baked goods a few miles to a small apartment complex on the western outskirt of the Cedar Springs city limits, where the Congolese refugees resided. Leaving her car running, she lifted the box of goods from the seat beside her, got out of the car, and quietly placed the box in front of one of the first-floor apartment units.

Just as Julie turned back toward her car, she was startled by the sound of the apartment door opening. Six-year-old Marie appeared in the doorway wearing pink fleece pajamas and silently waved at her. Julie wondered why she was up so early. Marie then said, "Good morning, Julie!" in a voice that seemed extra loud in the pre-dawn silence.

Julie smiled, stepped back to the door, leaned down, and hugged Marie tight. She whispered, "Hi, Marie. Have a good day, okay?"

Marie nodded, then Julie helped her slide the box inside the door and they waved goodbye to each other.

As Julie got back in her car, a fire engine with its siren blaring roared past on the two-lane highway. Whenever she heard sirens, she immediately wondered whether Eric or Beth were involved in the response. She glanced after the fire truck and thought she could see a faint orange glow through the darkness, over the trees in the distance. She knew Harriet's property and large house were in that vicinity. Curious, she started to turn onto the highway with the intention of following the fire truck in the direction of Harriet's house. She suddenly caught herself, thinking in surprisingly and unusually paranoid terms. She reasoned if the fire in the distance somehow involved Harriet's house, it would not be prudent of Julie to be seen there with the pending Christmas lights trial, lest she be suspected of some kind of crazy revenge arson. She silently thanked God for the cautionary realization, then turned left out of the apartment complex heading back toward downtown.

While Julie, Bev, Bonnie, and Teresa prepped the café to open for the day, Julie resisted the urge to wake Beth to see if she knew anything about the fire yet. Minutes later however, Beth actually called Julie with news from Eric that the fire was indeed at Harriet's house. Eric even helped carry an unconscious Harriet out of the burning house. Beth added that Eric said Harriet was quite heavy—a detail Julie found a bit inappropriately superfluous, though darkly humorous. Beth said Harriet was in the hospital with moderate burns but had regained consciousness. "Eric said her house is completely destroyed," Beth concluded.

Julie secretly repented of the thought flashing through her mind, that Harriet might have set fire to her own house to collect the insurance money (particularly if Harriet was as broke as Beth related the night before).

Julie shared the tragic news about Harriet with Bev and
Bonnie who were equally astonished. Their conversation was interrupted by the arrival of the morning's first customers, so Julie
set about her tasks, though her mind was very much elsewhere.
The thought was rather unpleasant, but it was too dominant for
her to ignore: *she had to go visit Harriet in the hospital.*

Perry arrived at the SB&C mid-morning. He looked and
felt stronger every day, and with Christmas just two days away,
there was a spring in his step the family had not seen since before
his heart attack. He felt like working a while, so Julie seized the
opportunity to drive to the hospital on the other side of town.
Before leaving, she called Pastor Tim, who had already heard
the news about Harriet from another parishioner, and he readily
agreed to Julie's request to meet her at the hospital.

✳ ✳ ✳

When Julie and Pastor Tim arrived at the hospital, they
asked to visit Harriet, which seemed to surprise the middle-aged
female attendant at the reception desk in the lobby. She quickly
suppressed her shock and inquired whether they were members
of Harriet's family. Since they were decidedly *not* family, the attendant said she would call the nurses' station to find out if Harriet would allow visitors. Julie and Tim waited silently while she
made the brief call, only to find out that Harriet was receiving
treatment and they would have to inquire again later. They said
they would wait awhile and thanked her for her help.

Just as they turned to leave the desk, the attendant stood,
leaned toward them, and in a hushed tone as if she was about to
share secret information said, "You know, in all the times Ms.

Paddock has been here over the years, I think you're the first visitors she's ever had."

"Is that right?" asked Pastor Tim, exchanging a concerned look with Julie.

The attendant wondered whether Harriet had any relatives in the area. Based on what Julie had gleaned from Beth, she said she didn't think so, but no one seemed to really know very much about Harriet. From there, after learning Tim was a pastor, the lady digressed into a long diatribe on how she used to be a member at Tim's church before he became pastor there, followed by far too much detail concerning the positives and mostly negatives of every church she'd attended since. Julie appreciated the graceful patience exhibited by Pastor Tim, a discipline no doubt honed from years of enduring similarly tedious rants.

Finally, Julie and Tim found an opening to take their leave and relocate to the waiting room where they would linger a few more minutes in case the opportunity to visit Harriet materialized. They chatted about her dad's health and her approaching voyage until Pastor Tim's buzzing phone interrupted them. He tugged it out of his front pocket and checked the screen.

"It's Jeanine. I better take this," he said. "Excuse me a minute."

Julie nodded—Jeanine was the church's beloved long-time secretary. Tim stepped out of the waiting room and around a corner to the adjacent vending machine nook.

Julie glanced at the only other people sitting in the quiet waiting room, a young couple half-heartedly watching the television while a boy who looked to be preschool age played with Matchbox cars on the floor at their feet. Pastor Tim's phone conversation took several minutes, so while waiting for him to return, Julie took out her own phone and checked the weather in London. Then she began typing reminders of last-minute trip details to take care of.

Tim reappeared in the doorway and Julie looked up from her phone.

"Can we talk out here for a minute?" he asked.

Julie slipped her phone in her back pocket and quickly joined him just outside the waiting room.

"Jeanine just got a call at the church from a woman named Karla who says she used to work part-time for Harriet, helping her with household chores and things."

"Sounds like the worst job ever," Julie interjected. She almost immediately regretted her joke timing, even if it *was* true.

"Apparently this lady had to quit a few months ago because Harriet's checks started bouncing. Harriet couldn't pay her anymore. She says she doesn't know how Harriet ever paid her anything because Harriet has so many unpaid medical bills from cancer treatments a few years back. Karla says bill collectors used to call all the time. She says she knows Harriet owes tens of thousands of dollars at least, because there were always piles of bills laying around the house."

Julie closed her eyes and winced.

"So, when she heard about Harriet's house burning down this morning, she felt like she had to do something," continued Pastor Tim. "She didn't know who else to call, so she tried the church. She said Harriet doesn't have a friend in the world and she's mean as hell, but she still didn't want her to end up living under an overpass or something."

Julie shook her head sympathetically. "It's so sad. I've never seen anyone so disliked and alone." Tears formed in her eyes.

"Me neither."

"I always thought Harriet had everything together. I always just bought the narrative that she was super wealthy."

"I know. Well…" He stared at the floor a moment, thinking. "I can talk to the church elders Sunday. Maybe we can figure out a way to help."

Julie nodded, glimpsing the television in the waiting room out of the corner of her eye. She glanced at the young couple who were now gazing into their phones. The little boy on the floor stared up at the TV screen, watching, at least for a moment, *It's a Wonderful Life*. Julie shook her head slightly—*what else could it be?* she thought. She watched the black & white footage for a moment. She was briefly confused, observing what appeared to be George Bailey repeatedly slugging the Mr. Potter character in the mid-section. Finally, it dawned on her this was not a scene from *It's a Wonderful Life* at all, but an old *Saturday Night Live* parody sketch with Dana Carvey as George Bailey. Nevertheless, the scene suddenly jolted Julie with an idea. It was radical, it made her slightly queasy, and yet she was flooded with the sense it was absolutely right.

She turned back toward Pastor Tim. "I can't believe it. I think I know what I'm supposed to do."

"What's wrong?"

"Nothing. But I've got to go. Can I meet you back here in an hour?"

"Sure. Everything all right?"

"Yes…I know how we can help Harriet." With that, she rushed down the hall and out of the hospital to her car.

✳ ✳ ✳

Julie drove back home, breaking every speed limit en route and hoping Beth was not patrolling the streets with her radar gun. She started to bound up the stairs to her flat, but an uneasy slip on the thin layer of snow and ice covering the steps made her slow down for the rest of the climb. Once inside, she rushed to the sock drawer in her bedroom and retrieved her checkbook.

Next, she drove to Shelly's where she grabbed a Christmas card from the rack near the register—the one with the photograph of the Cedar Springs bridge covered in Christmas lights and snow. She hurriedly greeted a few customers, then gave her parents and Bonnie the *Reader's Digest* version of Harriet's circumstances. She was vague about her exact reason for returning to the hospital, saying only that she and Pastor Tim had not yet been able to visit with Harriet.

Sitting back in her parked car behind the café, Julie carefully filled out a check payable to Harriet Paddock. Next, she wrote a brief message inside the Christmas card:

> *No man (or woman!) is an island.*
>
> *I Timothy 1:12-17*

Then she signed her name, tucked the check inside the card, and wrote "Harriet" on the front of the envelope.

She drove back to the hospital, hewing closer to the speed limits this time, with a feverish sense of joy and anticipation. She could not explain it, but she felt confident it was God urging her on. A peace swelled in her heart and mind that was beyond her comprehension and confirmed her plan.

While Julie was on her mystery errand, Pastor Tim bought a bouquet of flowers for Harriet from the hospital gift shop. Julie complimented his choice of arrangement when they reconvened at the reception desk in the lobby. The chatty attendant called the nurses' station once again requesting permission for Julie and Tim to visit Harriet. Julie mostly expected Harriet to deny the request, and her palms dampened while they awaited the verdict. Finally, to Julie's surprise and slight dread, the attendant gave them the go-ahead to proceed to Harriet's room. Before they could escape the desk however, they endured one more protracted soliloquy from the attendant on the perils of online shopping. Eventually, they wriggled free and with the card and flowers in tow, proceeded to Harriet's room.

As they reached the closed door of Harriet's room, Julie took a deep breath. She looked hesitantly at Pastor Tim who nodded at her reassuringly. He knocked rather softly and they paused until they heard Harriet's gruff, unmistakable voice impatiently reply: "What now?"

Tim opened the door to find Harriet, sitting up in bed, wearily picking at a lunch tray. Bandages covered portions of Harriet's forearms and neck. She barely glanced up at them as they crossed the small room to the foot of her bed.

"Oh, Lord. I was afraid of this. Look, Pastor, you seem nice and all, but don't think I'm going to run to your church now just because everything I own burned up. The Lord giveth and the Lord taketh away. But in my experience, he mostly taketh away, so we're not on speaking terms."

Several potential retorts occurred to Julie and she was certain Pastor Tim could muster some more nuanced retorts of his own, but she was glad he opted for the high road. "How are you feeling, Harriet?" he asked.

"I'd be a hell of a lot better if this hospital food wasn't such crap." She dropped her fork on the tray in frustration. Pastor Tim took it as an opportunity to extend the flower bouquet toward her.

"These are for you," he offered.

Harriet barely turned her head to see the flowers and scoffed. "Just put them over there with all the others," she said sarcastically.

Julie and Pastor Tim glanced around. There was not a single flower anywhere in the room.

"Now I suppose you want me to make a donation to the church or something?" continued Harriet.

"That won't be necessary," he replied.

"And what's *your* excuse for being here?" asked Harriet, briefly cutting her eyes toward Julie. "Come to finish me off?"

Julie expected such a barb. "Actually, we just wanted to bring you a gift to help out. I know it can't replace losing your house, but maybe it can be a start." She held out the card toward Harriet who did not budge to accept it, so Julie set it next to the tray beneath Harriet's skeptical scowl.

"Honey, I'm the wealthiest person in the county. What makes you think I need *your* help?"

It was such an odd, awkward protest, even from Harriet, that Julie felt pity for her.

"Let me guess," continued Harriet, "the whole town pitched in for a gift card to Home Depot. Since I'm such a beloved figure and all."

Julie and Pastor Tim exchanged brief glances, their sympathy mutually roused, but neither sure what to say. Harriet was the embodiment of bitterness.

"So, will that be all?" snapped Harriet.

"Uh, yes, I suppose. But we can stay and keep you company for a while if you'd like," Julie offered.

"That won't be necessary," said Harriet.

Julie and Pastor Tim exchanged uncertain glances again. Julie hoped Harriet would at least open the card, but it did not look like that was in the offing.

"Okay, well," said Pastor Tim, "I guess we'll be on our way."

"I guess so," agreed Julie. "Hope you feel better soon, Harriet."

Harriet picked up her fork and stabbed at a carrot. "I'm sure you do."

Julie and Pastor Tim left the room and walked in silence toward the main lobby. Finally, in a near whisper, Julie said, "Well, that was…" but she could not muster any apt descriptors.

"About what you'd expect from Harriet," he said.

"Right."

Outside the hospital entrance, the sky was densely overcast as if pondering more snow in time for Christmas. Julie thanked Pastor Tim for joining her and hugged him before they diverged to their respective cars. Julie drove back to Shelly's where she hoped to take Perry's place at work and convince him to go home for a nap.

As Julie drove back to the SB&C, she smiled at the thought of Harriet's eyes widening and jaw dropping when she saw the check. She hoped Harriet would not simply rip it up and prayed it would help chip away at Harriet's stone heart. Julie's heart ached for Harriet now that she understood the source of her pain. She could not discard the picture in her mind of an eight-year-old Harriet, all alone, assaulted by the twin miseries of losing both her parents at Christmas.

Suddenly, a sinking, painful, doubting feeling flooded Julie and she wondered if she had done something entirely foolish. She had diligently saved for ten years to finance her world travels. *Was it idiotic of her to give so much of it away? Especially to her archenemy? Had she done the right thing?*

In human terms, she supposed it *was* rather idiotic—that is why she could not tell a soul how much she gave. But in spiritual terms, she was at peace with the decision. In fact, in light of God's grace, it seemed like the least she could do.

Julie was still determined to leave on her trip the day after Christmas, but she was already editing her previous master travel plan in her mind. Her donation to Harriet meant New Zealand would now have to be cut. She figured she would limit herself to Europe, since her first flight was already booked for London. She estimated her remaining $15,000 in travel savings would buy her a few months in Europe if she stretched every penny. It would no longer be a year around the world, but she thought three months in Europe still sounded rather grand for a gal who had barely been out of North Carolina.

Chapter 22

A small rectangular sign hanging in the SB&C's front door window read: *CHRISTMAS EVE – CLOSING AT NOON*. It was a wooden, hand-painted sign Julie made when she was twelve and which her parents used every Christmas Eve since.

The Shellys always remained open on Christmas Eve morning, more as a service to the community than for any real profit margin. Many Cedar Springs citizens simply enjoyed it as a part of the Christmas tradition, a gathering place to share in the buzz and anticipation of the holiday. Perry, Bev, Aunt Bonnie, Teresa, and Julie were all at the café, though the occasion felt more like a celebration than work.

Bev tried to convince Julie she should go home and pack for her trip, but Julie would not have missed work on Christmas Eve. Plus, she had not yet told her parents about giving three-quarters of her trip money to Harriet. She was apprehensive about telling them and seriously considering waiting until she was in Europe to do so. The reality of her departure in less than forty-eight hours brought pangs of nervousness, anticipation, and melancholy as the idea of actually leaving her family for a few months began to sink in.

Mid-morning, Beth arrived in her police uniform for her customary coffee break. She sat at the counter and Julie hurried over with a tall mug of coffee made just the way Beth liked it. Beth took one long sip before she divulged the real reason for her visit. She had a good-natured bone to pick with Julie.

"I know about the money," she began cryptically, in a hushed tone.

Julie could not suppress a deer-in-headlights expression. *How could Beth possibly know?* "What?" she protested innocently.

"Don't play innocent with me, missy!" continued Beth. "How could you even think of doing that? You've practically been saving for this trip since high school!"

"Shhh!" Julie nodded sideways toward her parents. "They don't know yet. And how the heck did *you* find out?"

"Sources. Note the badge?" Beth flicked the police insignia on her coat.

"Whatever. Seriously, how'd you find out?"

"From Joey who patrols the hospital."

"How the heck did *he* find out?"

"He said one of the nurses was in Harriet's room when Harriet opened your card and found the check. The nurse said Harriet swore like a sailor at first but then just started sobbing uncontrollably. And when the nurse tried to console her, Harriet showed her the check for $45,000. Anyway, that nurse told Joey all about it."

"For heaven's sake, the gossip around here sometimes."

"Just *sometimes*? According to Joey, Harriet is telling everyone that comes near her room about the insane life-saving gift from Julie Shelly."

Julie shook her head slowly. "I really didn't know how she would react."

"Come on, how long did you think you could keep that a secret? You think nobody was going to wonder why you didn't leave on this trip you've been talking about forever?"

"Oh, I'm still going. It'll just have to be, you know, about nine months shorter than I planned."

"You should've consulted me first. I would've told you to forget it. I mean, maybe I could understand if it was anyone besides Harriet. But she's never lifted a finger to help a soul! If the situation was reversed, she would never help you."

"You *have* been introduced to the doctrine of *grace*, right?" Julie teased. "I thought you'd understand better than anyone."

"Nope. Sorry. You've worked so hard. *This is your dream.* I could understand like a thousand bucks, maybe. But *that* much? What were you thinking?"

"Everything just started to make sense. All this weirdness with the movie and the card and everything."

"Huh?" Beth looked puzzled.

"Van said something the other day that really struck me— that maybe all this stuff isn't about me. So then I'm standing in the waiting room at the hospital yesterday and guess what was on the TV?"

"*Mary Poppins,*" said Beth sarcastically.

Julie continued, ignoring Beth's incorrect guess. "It was this old SNL parody where what's-his-name is playing George Bailey and they go get revenge on Mr. Potter and beat him up. And I can relate, you know, to wishing some ill toward Harriet."

Skepticism covered Beth's face and she shifted uncomfortably on the stool.

"But now life is kicking Harriet, as hard as it can," continued Julie. "And if I revel in that, even for a second, then I'm just as miserable as she is. It couldn't have been clearer. It was like a big glowing sign."

"A sign of *what?*" demanded Beth.

"That this was a crossroads for me. A life-defining test. It's easy to help out people you like. But what about someone you can't stand? I'm supposed to love my enemies, but do I really? All of a sudden Harriet didn't seem like my enemy anymore. All I could see was the eight-year-old Harriet. Alone on Christmas Day, not knowing why or where her mother had gone. And then her father killing himself. And the next Christmas, with both of her parents gone. Van was right. It's *not* all about me. I think it was about Harriet. Maybe everything that's happened was just to get me to the point of helping her. It's kind of a liberating feeling in an odd way. The mystery's solved."

"I'm sorry, I don't know what to think about the weird *Wonderful Life* stuff. But it's probably nothing. Look, sometimes good stuff happens, sometimes bad stuff happens. But in the end, it's all just random stuff that happens. We look for deeper meaning to help us cope with the randomness. And as far as Harriet goes, yeah, I feel sorry for eight-year-old Harriet too. But elderly Harriet could make different choices. She *could* decide not to be such a miserable jerk."

"I get what you're saying. I really do. But I'm at peace with the decision."

"Aren't you sad your dream trip is off though? *I'm* sad about it and I wasn't even going anywhere."

"It's not off! I'm going to Europe for three months. How many people get to do that?"

Beth leaned across the counter and embraced Julie. "You are truly something, you know that?" asked Beth.

"Nah. If I was truly something, I would've given away *all* my money. I'm still going to Europe."

They laughed and released each other. "Did she at least say thank you?"

"No," replied Julie, with a slight shake of her head.

"Drop the lawsuit?"

"Nope."

"Unbelievable. She's like Scrooge and Mr. Potter combined. *Scrotter*."

Julie grinned at her friend's lovely dorkiness. She glimpsed Van looking in the front window and waved at him. He bounded inside and Julie walked around to join Van and Beth on their side of the counter.

"Hey!" greeted Julie.

"Hey! Merry Christmas," said Van.

"Merry Christmas to you! So…the interview?"

Van's face fell a little. "Yeah, well, for some reason they decided to go in a different direction…and hire *me*."

"Van, that's amazing!" Julie hugged him.

Beth eyed them and grinned.

Julie let go of Van as another reality set in. "It's amazing except the part where you move away and we never see you again, of course."

"Yes. There is that small detail. I'm driving to my parents' for Christmas and after that I gotta hustle back here to pack up all my stuff. 'Cuz I guess I'm moving to Arkansas. I start the new job at the end of January."

Julie had a sudden, sinking feeling her failure to reciprocate when Van told her he loved her that night at the café might have actually caused him to pursue and accept this job. Now he was leaving.

Van tried to brush aside the encroaching sentiment. "You'll be having too much fun taking safari photos and stuff to miss me."

"I don't know about that."

"Well, I really gotta get going, but I had to stop in Shelly's one more time, grab a cup for the road."

Julie felt sharp tears begin to form, but she managed to keep them at bay by returning behind the counter and preparing Van's cup of coffee. As she did, Beth made small talk with Van about his new college assistant coaching job. Julie quickly rejoined them and handed Van the steaming cup.

"Thanks," he said as he took the coffee from her.

Julie held up some napkins. "Emergency napkins."

"Do you know me, or what?" he replied, his fingers brushing hers as he accepted the napkins. Their eyes met for a fleeting moment. He took a deep breath. "Well. Goodbyes are the worst. So…I guess it's *the worst* for now."

Julie could not bring herself to say 'bye.' "Okay, have a safe trip. And a good Christmas. Say 'hi' to your parents for me."

"Will do," said Van as he went in for another embrace. It was a longer one this time.

Julie closed her eyes. Saying *I love you* was on the very tip of her tongue. The words were on the verge of tumbling out, but she pulled the plug at the last possible second. She thought it wouldn't be fair to him, to drop such a bombshell as he was on his way out the door. She was two days from leaving the country. He was taking a job in another state. If there was a window of opportunity for them to be more than friends, she had missed it. In the pressure of the moment, it just didn't seem prudent to try to force that window back open now. So, with great difficulty, she swallowed the words.

"Take care of yourself," he said sincerely, leaning his head against hers.

Julie could no longer hide the tears filling her eyes, but she formed a quivering smile as she said, "You too."

They finally let go.

"See ya, Beth," said Van, as a casual way to aid his exit.

"See ya, Van," replied Beth, with as much cheer as she could muster for Julie's sake.

Van lifted his hand in Julie's direction just as he walked out the café door. Julie lifted her hand in return and watched him go.

"Do you have to work tonight?" Julie asked, lamely and quickly trying to change the subject.

"Actually no. Thank God! First time in three years I've been off Christmas Eve," replied Beth.

"Are you going to the Christmas Eve service then?"

"We'll be there."

"Cool."

Julie stared out the front windows again. Beth stood, draped her right arm across Julie's shoulders, and asked, "So how long have you been in love with Van?"

Julie wiped a tear from her face. She grinned at Beth for a second. "I'm not sure exactly." She quickly ducked out from under her friend's arm. "But I can't really deal with it right now."

Julie returned behind the counter to busy herself and avoid any of Beth's potential follow-up questions.

Fortunately, a welcome distraction came just after the family closed the café at noon, when Hugh and Robyn arrived for Christmas. They announced to the family their selection of July

18th for their wedding date. Without explaining to her family how and why she would be cutting short her international journey, Julie assured Hugh and Robyn she would be able to make it to their wedding, which they planned to have in Cedar Springs.

After catching up with Hugh and Robyn, Julie spent the late afternoon in her flat, wrapping Christmas gifts. She never quite mastered her mom's art of actually wrapping presents in time for them to be displayed under the tree several days before Christmas. Julie's Christmas Eve wrapping process habitually took much longer than she anticipated. The job was prolonged by the fact she interspersed it with packing and general trip preparation. Whenever a trip-related task came to mind, she immediately paused the gift-wrapping job to take care of the task right away before she forgot.

She sat on the floor in front of her couch surrounded by rolls of wrapping paper, tape, ribbon, and scissors. Christmas music from WPVS played on the radio. She put the finishing touches on a wrapped gift for her dad, a large book about Calvin Coolidge. Perry was always the most difficult family member to buy presents for because he never seemed to want anything. Julie loved that about him though, and was confident he would enjoy a nerdy, weighty tome about Coolidge whom she knew to be his second-favorite president after George Washington.

When she finished wrapping the book, she leaned back against the couch and gazed at her modest pile of presents. The Beach Boys' version of "I'll Be Home for Christmas" began on the radio. The slow, heavily harmonized rendition gave the song an extra dose of melancholy. She sighed deeply and reached for her camera bag on the couch behind her—the early Christmas gift from the mystery-giver that she received at Cedar Springs Camera Supply on Black Friday. She removed the camera from the bag, looked through the lens and snapped a shot of the gift pile. She figured she should continue packing the suitcase and backpack which lay on her bed in total disarray, but she suddenly felt weary and procrastinated.

Instead, she put the camera back in its bag and picked up the London travel guide from the lamp table beside the couch, flipping aimlessly through its worn, dog-eared pages. A knock on the door interrupted her frazzled thoughts.

"Come in!" said Julie.

Bev opened the door and entered carrying a large, flat, rectangular gift-wrapped box. "Hey, sweetie. I forgot to tell you Van Beal dropped this off for you yesterday."

"Really?" Julie stood to check it out.

"I think it's a Christmas gift," said Bev, winking at Julie.

"Good guess, Mom."

Julie took the unwieldy package from her mom and tore off the paper. She pried open the cardboard box, then carefully pulled out a framed, full-size *It's a Wonderful Life* movie poster. She beamed and held it up proudly for Bev to admire.

Bev's smile faded slightly. "Wise-guy. That's not funny."

"It's *perfect*," said Julie, as she set the framed poster on the floor by the couch, leaning it against her bookcase. As she did so, the old Christmas card with the Cedar Springs bridge on the front caught her eye and she picked it up from the bookshelf. She read the inside of the card again to herself:

December 25, 1986

Dear Julie,

You truly have the most amazing life.
Thank you for giving me hope.

Love,
Gwen

Bev watched her daughter curiously. Julie sat back down on the edge of the couch. She studied the bridge on the front of the card, stared at the movie poster, then back to the card. She was suddenly struck with the memory of that strange dream, in which she stood alone on the bridge looking for something. With the lights flashing. And the blizzard blowing in. And that car almost hitting her. *Why was she on the bridge in her dream, and what was she looking for?*

"What's wrong?"

"Nothing," replied Julie, springing off the couch again, "But I've got to go."

"Where? You're going to the candle-light service, right?"

"Yeah, I'll meet you there. I just have to take care of something first." Julie hurried around, gathering her coat, mittens, hat, and scarf.

"Are you okay?"

Julie threw the brakes on her harried activity, hugged Bev tight, and kissed her cheek. "Absolutely!" She looked her mom in the eyes for emphasis. "I promise."

As soon as Bev left to return home, Julie resumed her frenzied preparation, suddenly on a mission. She quickly made hot cocoa on the stove, with actual whole milk (*after all*, she told herself, *it was Christmas Eve*). She poured the hot cocoa into the shiny silver thermos Hugh gave her for Christmas a few years back, but which she rarely had occasion to use.

She grabbed her two fleece blankets and her sleeping bag, and with car keys and thermos in hand, walked carefully down the snow-covered stairs. Mild snow flurries waltzed on a light, frosty wind. She was glad to see snow but relieved nothing was freezing to her windshield yet. She put the blankets, sleeping bag, and thermos in her car, then slipped quietly into her parents' garage and reemerged with a collapsible camping chair in its drawstring carrying bag, which she placed in her car's trunk. Then she got in the car and backed slowly out of the driveway.

As soon as she shifted the car into drive, she almost talked herself out of what she feared was probably a silly venture. Yet she felt an unusual peace, and something almost like a quiet voice in her mind urging her on. She hoped that that *something* was God, though it was admittedly hard for her to believe. It was a peaceful feeling quite similar to how she felt when she was on the way to the hospital with the gift for Harriet. But this feeling was even stronger—peace, interwoven with joy. She hoped it was God, otherwise she would not be able to overpower the familiar, lingering dread she could actually be losing her mind. She comforted herself with self-soothing logic that people who lose their mind surely are not conscious of the fact when they are in the process.

It was already dark, with few cars on the streets. She prayed if this was not a God-sanctioned trip, He would somehow inspire her to turn back. Nothing broke the silence, and her joyful peace persisted. So, she drove on.

Chapter 23

On the eastern edge of downtown Cedar Springs, just before the red, steel-truss bridge, there was a small parking alcove with a handful of spaces. The spaces were almost always filled when the weather was nice, as the spot was within relatively easy walking distance of downtown and provided access to a scenic spot with safety railing overlooking the river below. Since it was already after dark on Christmas Eve, the parking alcove was abandoned, a fact which relieved Julie as she turned into the lot and slipped into the first space.

She sat in her car with the engine still running, savoring the heat wafting through the vents. The car thermometer indicated it was twenty-nine degrees outside. After a couple of minutes, she finally turned off the car. In the sudden silence, she could hear the wet snowflakes, already a bit heavier since she left home, pitter-pattering against the windshield. She could also hear the steady rush of the river flowing over the boulders and down two steep cascades just below the overlook, near where she sat.

She stared out the windshield at the bridge, without any idea what she was really looking for. She felt self-conscious again and wished she had invited Beth along on this curious stake-out. In an effort to justify her unusual circumstance, she shuffled through the evidence in her mind that led her to this point. The sprinkler incident that doused the crowd at the *It's a Wonderful Life*-themed fundraiser. Mike and his family living in the old Gilroy house. Hugh returning home with a fiancée. Harriet maintaining her status as the Shelly family's perennial, miserly nemesis. Van nearly falling through the ice and Julie saving him. Her discovery of the old family photo of her grandmother with Jimmy Stewart and Frank Capra. Then there was the confounding arrival of that Christmas card and her stirring dream about the bridge. Bizarre as it seemed, the sum total of it all renewed her faith she was exactly where she was supposed to be.

She suddenly remembered another puzzle piece she had not considered before—the camera gift from a secret Santa reminded her of George Bailey receiving the new suitcase from Mr. Gower. All at once, she knew with rare certainty whom the camera was from…the movie poster was actually her *second* Christmas gift from Van. *He truly did love her.* The realization filled her eyes with tears in an instant swell that took her breath away.

After scrounging in her car for a tissue, she had to settle for a fast-food napkin she found in the driver's side door compartment. She dabbed her eyes and wiped her runny nose. She glanced at the bridge again, disappointed her full view of it was obscured by cedar trees and the location of the parking alcove down a short incline from street level. She wanted to be able to see the entire bridge.

Steeling herself for the cold, she opened the car door and stepped out into the falling snow with her thermos of hot cocoa. She retrieved her blankets, sleeping bag, and camping chair from the car and walked up the short flight of steps from the parking alcove to the sidewalk that led onto the bridge. She stopped at the start of the bridge and set up her camping chair on the sidewalk that was already covered by a half-inch of sugar-like snow. She sat in the chair and slid the sleeping bag over herself like a giant sock, then further wrapped her torso in the two fleece blankets. She sipped her hot cocoa from the thermos. *In all, not a terrible way to spend part of a Christmas Eve*, she thought.

As Julie discovered, Christmas Eve in Cedar Springs was an ideal time to do something odd in a public setting. With most folks preoccupied with family celebrations at home, the likelihood of one's curious behavior garnering notice, let alone being questioned, drastically diminished. Julie counted on the streets being mostly deserted after dark because she could not adequately explain her current enterprise.

It was 6:05 p.m., and snow descended in weighty clumps from the starless, black-matted sky. Julie knew she looked bizarre, like she was waiting for a parade to start or camping out in line for concert tickets. She felt inexplicably compelled to be there at that very moment, though the compulsion was not quite strong enough to chase away her potential embarrassment.

As a few cars traversed the narrow two-lane bridge at a leisurely holiday pace, Julie tried burrowing deeper into the canvas seat of her camping chair, as if it might help conceal her from the glow of the headlight beams. Some motorists noticed her; others did not, or at least pretended not to. She was rather hard to miss in her prominent seated position on the sidewalk that ran alongside the decades-old bridge railing. One car slowed as it approached, and she tensed with fear the driver would stop to ask questions. She instantly prepared a contingent reply to any inquiries. She would say she was "just enjoying the snow," or something similarly lame, which would be truthful without divulging the actual reason for her visit to the bridge. She made a snap decision to smile and wave enthusiastically at the craned-neck driver, figuring that might better discourage questioning than if she sat motionless, hoping not to be noticed. Fortunately, the car continued on its way.

Julie did not want to be interrogated because no rational explanation existed for why she sat by herself on the bridge in the freezing Christmas Eve air. The truth was that she was waiting for something to happen. She had no idea *what,* just the most persistent hunch it would be something *important.* The only similarly strong intuition she recalled having in her life was the time in fifth grade when she was almost certain she was going to get a full-size backyard trampoline for Christmas. Alas, no trampoline materialized.

Just as she was about to laugh off her intuition incompetence and rejoin the sane world, something *did* happen.

While Julie contemplated packing up her solo bridge-watch party, she began dozing. With the hot cocoa, the abundance of fleecy layers, and the soothing lull of the icy river cascading over the boulders directly below the bridge, her surroundings soon faded into a wintry fog. She resisted the first couple of head-bobs but quickly gave up the fight and drifted off.

Julie was only asleep for a couple of minutes when a pickup truck approached the opposite end of the bridge from where she sat. On that side of the river there was a bend in the road leading onto the bridge. The truck hurtled toward the sharp curve at a reckless speed. As the driver attempted to brake and maintain control through the curve, the truck hit an icy patch on the short straightaway before the bridge. The truck skidded off the road and its right front fender barreled into a large, ancient cedar tree just before the start of the bridge.

The violent, metallic clatter jolted Julie awake, her left leg involuntarily flailing in the process. Her eyes fluttered open and she brushed the wet snowflakes from her face. She leaned forward in her chair, momentarily disoriented, and surprised to realize she had fallen asleep. Glancing cautiously back and forth, she hoped no further passersby had witnessed her conked out on the bridge like that, as it would be impossible to explain her way out of that one.

Having regained her bearings, she peered straight ahead, squinting through the thickly falling snow across the bridge. She could make out a dingy blue and white pickup truck with its right front fender crumpled against the dense trunk of a majestic cedar tree, one of several such trees just off the shoulder of the road near the start of the bridge.

Julie stood, trying to gather her senses and find her phone. She checked her coat pockets, the camping chair, and the snow-caked concrete around her to no avail. *Perfect*, she thought, figuring she left it at home.

The unscathed driver's side door of the crashed pickup truck slowly opened with a rusty, drawn-out squeal, interrupting Julie's annoyance at forgetting her phone. As she watched, a haggard teenage girl tumbled out of the cab and fell to her knees in the snow. She lingered on the bitter cold ground for a moment, weeping loud enough for Julie to hear. The girl picked herself up and stumbled alongside the guardrail for several yards until she stepped onto the sidewalk of the bridge. Julie froze at the alarming scene unfolding in slow motion. In her sleepy stupor, Julie could not settle fast enough on the best course of action.

Oblivious to Julie's presence, the girl's deep, sorrowful crying persisted as she trudged aimlessly through the ankle-deep snow of the bridge's sidewalk. Julie noted the girl wore only a sweatshirt and jeans, which had to be scant protection against the night's biting cold. She stopped near the middle of the bridge and leaned over the railing, prompting Julie to shift forward uneasily in her chair. Beneath the bridge, the churning dark river surged over and around large, smooth boulders on its way toward the falls. The girl's shoulders convulsed with her breathless sobs. From Julie's vantage point, she assumed the girl must be feeling sick.

Julie looked around, suddenly hoping for a crowd. But the streets were empty and quiet, as if the town was taking a deep breath, finally about to allow itself a respite from all the frenetic Christmas preparations. Julie and the teenage girl remained the only two souls on the bridge.

Finally, Julie's habitual compassion overruled her hesitation. With a deep breath of her own, she stood, unfurled herself from the blankets, unzipped her sleeping bag, and piled them on the camping chair. Then she cautiously approached the grieving stranger. Between the din of the rushing river and her own weeping, the girl did not hear the crunch of snow underfoot as Julie crossed the bridge toward her.

Very slowly, as if each movement of her limbs sapped all of her energy, the teenage girl hoisted her torso on top of the bridge railing. She swung her right leg over the railing, then her left. Jolted with alarm at the sight of the girl now standing precariously on the narrow ledge overhanging the river, Julie jogged the rest of the way. Tears streamed down the girl's face as she stared at the rushing ice water below.

"Wait! Don't!" Julie exclaimed just before she reached the railing.

Startled, the girl's left foot slipped on the frozen ledge, but she grabbed the railing and steadied herself before letting go

again, her hands trembling. The girl was not wearing gloves and
Julie thought her hands must be nearly numb from the stinging,
wet cold. Panic consumed the teen's face as she glanced over her
shoulder at Julie, and then very slowly bent her knees, seemingly about to leap.

"No! Stop!" cried Julie desperately. Instinctively, she
reached out and clasped her hands around the girl's left upper
arm. Gently, but firmly, Julie pulled her back against the railing.
"Please don't. Please don't," said Julie, trembling only slightly
less than the girl.

The stranger twisted her neck to see who held her and their
eyes met for the first time. Julie did not recognize her. Even in
the dim lights of the bridge, she immediately noticed the teen's
right eye was swollen and nearly surrounded by a dark bruise.

Julie continued gripping the girl's arm with her left hand,
but risked letting go with her right hand just long enough to repo-
sition it on her right shoulder. She tried to hold her more secure-
ly, the girl's back now pressed against the railing. The trembling
teen seemed stunned to see someone else.

"Please, just let me go," said the girl, her voice shaking.

Julie hesitated, grasping for an adequate reply. From
their vantage point, the sound of the rushing water below was
fierce and urgent.

"I can't do that," replied Julie.

"You don't understand."

"Please, climb back over. Please let me help."

"I *can't*," the girl said emphatically.

"Yes, you can. I'll help you. It's okay. I promise I've got
you." Julie tightened her grip on the girl's arm and shoulder. The
girl looked down at the water again, then back at Julie.

Finally, slowly and utterly defeated, the teen allowed Julie to help her climb back over the railing to the bridge sidewalk. When both their feet were steadily planted on the snow-covered pavement, Julie held the girl in an embrace.

"Thank God. You scared me," said Julie.

Tears dripped again from the girl's face, mixing with the fresh specks of snow on the front of Julie's coat.

The girl wore ripped, acid-wash jeans, dingy white canvas high-top sneakers, and an old, baggy, teal-colored sweatshirt with a faded image of Snoopy on the front. She had dirty brown hair haphazardly pulled into a ponytail. Julie guessed her to be around sixteen.

The girl backed out of Julie's arms, slumped to the snow-covered sidewalk, and leaned against the cold railing. Julie was unsure what to do next, especially with the girl's truck lodged against a tree.

"I'm just going to grab a blanket. I'll be right back." Julie was afraid to risk leaving the girl's side, but the teen shivered relentlessly. So, Julie jogged back to her camping chair, retrieved both blankets, returned, and draped the blankets over the girl's shoulders. Then she slowly sat beside her and they remained silent for several moments.

Finally, Julie thought of something to offer. "Do you feel like going inside? I know where we can find a warm fireplace and a hot drink. How does that sound?"

The girl closed her eyes tightly and Julie could not tell whether she further disturbed the teenager or offered a semblance of hope.

"It's really close by," pressed Julie.

With her eyes still shut, the girl swallowed strenuously, then reluctantly nodded. Julie helped the stranger to her feet, and with her right hand lightly resting on the girl's back, they walked slowly across the bridge toward Julie's car.

Chapter 24

Julie waffled over whether they should just walk from the bridge to the SB&C or take her car. She was hesitant to say or do anything, as she did not want to further upset the precarious stranger. Since they were walking right past her camping chair, sleeping bag, and thermos however, Julie went ahead and collected them. She hoped the girl would not inquire about the items as Julie had no idea how to explain without sounding like a lunatic. The teen remained silent, however, except for the sound of her sniffling and wiping her runny nose with the sleeve of her threadbare sweatshirt.

When they reached the end of the bridge, Julie guided the girl down the short set of steps to the parking alcove. Julie had left her car unlocked so she opened the front passenger door for the girl, then quickly set the camping chair, sleeping bag, and thermos in the backseat and hustled around to the driver's side. She wanted to get away from the bridge before the teen changed her mind and returned to the ledge.

The drive was brief, as Shelly's was barely half a mile away. As they rode in silence, Julie stole a few glances at the silent passenger. Her brown hair was a tangled mess, but Julie could see she was naturally quite pretty.

From the small parking area behind the café, the girl followed Julie inside through the back entrance that led into the kitchen. Julie continued into the café, turned on a couple lights, and lit the gas fireplace. The flickering fire coupled with the strands of Christmas lights in the front windows furnished a calming Christmas Eve ambience.

The teenager sat timidly on the edge of the fireplace with her back to the fire, still wrapped in Julie's two blankets. Julie's heart already ached for her guest, and she wished she could summarily lift the heavy burden so obvious in her downcast eyes and slumped shoulders. In the firelight, Julie got another glimpse of the purplish-black bruise around the girl's swollen right eye.

"Can I get you some ice for your eye?" ventured Julie.

The girl looked at the floor, mulling the offer. She seemed embarrassed, but finally nodded and Julie disappeared into the kitchen for a plastic bag, a handful of ice from the ice machine, and a clean hand towel, which she wrapped tightly around the ice bag. She briskly returned to the stranger's side and handed her the icepack, which the girl placed gingerly on her eye.

Neither of them knew what to say, but Julie figured the burden was on her to carry the conversation, so she said, "I'll go start some hot cocoa."

She hurried behind the counter and began warming up the milk, keeping a concerned eye on the teen as she worked. The girl glanced briefly around the café, but mostly stared emptily at the floor.

"I'm Julie by the way. My family owns this place." Julie paused for any sign of interest, but the girl barely looked in Julie's direction. "It's been around since 1946. That's when my grandparents started it."

The girl adjusted the ice on her eye.

"Do you like whipped cream in your cocoa...I'm sorry, what's your name?"

The girl shifted uneasily on the fireplace, pulling the blankets tighter around her with her left hand.

"Gwen Barnes."

"Nice to meet you, Gwen." As soon as she heard herself say the name aloud, Julie almost gasped, remembering the Christmas card. A sharp chill rushed up Julie's arms and neck. The startling realization caused her to tip over one of the mugs as she poured the milk, spilling cocoa across the counter. She quickly lunged for a towel to mop the mess, and as she did, glanced up at the girl. "*Gwen?*" she asked to confirm.

"Yeah?"

Julie resumed pouring the milk and stirring in the cocoa powder. "That's just really strange because I got this Christmas card in the mail a couple weeks ago and it was signed 'Gwen.' And I don't know anyone named Gwen. Well, until now. You wouldn't happen to know anything about that would you?"

Gwen did not seem to understand what Julie was implying. "No. I've never sent a Christmas card to anyone."

Julie walked around the counter carrying two mugs of hot cocoa. "Hmm. Well, anyway, it couldn't have been from you. It was lost in the mail for like, thirty years. It was weird." She sat on the fireplace on Gwen's left, careful not to sit too close and risk making Gwen feel more uncomfortable than Julie could tell she already felt. She handed Gwen one of the mugs. "So where are you from?"

Again, Gwen hesitated before answering, "Close to Asheville. Are you gonna call the cops?"

"I wasn't planning on it," replied Julie before she remembered it *had* crossed her mind to call Beth. "Are you in any kind of trouble?"

"Sort of. Yeah." Gwen stared at the floor again for several moments before adding, "I'm pregnant."

Julie was not prepared for Gwen's reply. "Oh." She hesitated to inquire about the circumstances of this development but decided to anyway. "How far along are you?" Julie glanced at Gwen's mid-section, but Gwen's baggy sweatshirt concealed any potential baby bump.

Gwen shrugged. "A few months I think." She took a slow sip of her cocoa. She winced a moment before staring at the floor again. "I really don't think you can help me, so…"

"I'm sorry. I'm just trying to make conversation. Honestly, I'm really not that great at small talk. My Aunt Bonnie on the other hand. She can out small talk anyone. Are you visiting family here, or…"

"No. I…I was just driving to get away. I don't really have anywhere to go. I just started driving."

"What about your parents?"

"My mom's in prison. Drugs. Don't know where my dad is. My stepdad did this." Gwen turned her head slightly toward Julie and lowered the ice pack from her swollen eye.

"I'm so sorry."

Tears glistened in Gwen's eyes again. "He found out about this…" she touched her stomach with the ice pack in her right hand. "Then he kicked me out. Told me not to come back until I got it taken care of. I don't want to live with him anyway. I just don't have anyone else."

Julie's mind raced and compassion flooded her heart for Gwen's desperate situation. She cringed at the thought but could not help wondering if Gwen's stepfather had abused her beyond the punches. Hesitantly, Julie asked, "What about the father of…"

"He's a total jerk. He's gone too. I was afraid to tell him when I found out I was pregnant. I knew he'd disappear. I was right. He said it's not his. But I know it is. He's twenty-two. He's a truck driver. He won't be coming back."

Gwen set her mug on the fireplace to wipe at new tears with her sleeve. "I can't take care of a baby. I can barely take care of myself. I don't want it. Nobody wants me neither. I just think…what's the point of anything? No one cares. They say they do. But no one really does. I just thought it would be easier if I wasn't here anymore. Maybe God would forgive me. If there is a God. And then I wouldn't have to live through this hell anymore. I know it's all my fault. I could've told him no. I wanted to. But then I just…"

Julie reached out and put her hand on Gwen's shoulder.

"You don't have to pretend to like me. No one else does," said Gwen. "Only thing worse than a white trash girl is one who's pregnant."

"I'm not pretending."

"You don't even know me. Nobody's *that* nice."

"Well, you've never met my parents."

"My stepdad's gonna kill me anyway when he finds out his truck's gone."

"Maybe I can help you figure something out."

Gwen resumed drinking her hot cocoa and they gazed out the front windows of the café. People were walking toward the courthouse square. Gwen and Julie were silent for a moment, then Julie ventured an explanation for the small crowd beginning to file past outside.

"People are starting to show up for the candlelight service in the square. We have it every Christmas Eve." Julie stood with her mug, hoping Gwen would follow her to the windows. Slowly, with one blanket still wrapped around her, Gwen joined Julie at the window.

"There goes Pastor Tim and his wife, Maggie," said Julie, gesturing out the window, "They're the best. They'll do anything for anybody."

A few of the Congolese refugee families approached on the café side of Main Street. Julie explained her church was helping them resettle here after they escaped the warzone in their home country. "Their resilience is incredible," said Julie. The families waved when they saw Julie standing in the café window. Six-year-old Marie jogged over to the window in front of Julie, pressed her nose into the glass, smiled widely, and waved with abandon. Julie pressed her nose against the glass and waved in reply.

Julie and Gwen continued people-watching at the window. "That's Jim. He owns this great camera shop down the street. I like photography, so sometimes he displays some of my photos. Not that they're all that great, Jim's just a nice guy. And that's my best friend, Beth, with her husband Eric. She's a police officer and he's a fireman."

Gwen lowered the ice pack from her eye for a better view.

"Need some more ice?" asked Julie.

Gwen shook her head and sipped her drink. On the sidewalk across the street from Shelly's, Beth and Eric laughed and held hands as they walked.

"Beth and Eric are hilarious," Julie continued, "They already bicker like an old couple. But in a good way. They totally love each other."

Beth noticed Julie in the window and held up her hands questioningly, wondering what Julie was doing and who the unidentified girl was beside her. Julie held up a finger to indicate she would join them shortly. Beth gave her thumbs up and continued with Eric toward the square.

Julie could not tell if her rambling on about her friends annoyed Gwen, but Gwen did not seem disinterested, so Julie continued. "Here comes my family! That's my brother, Hugh, and his fiancée, Robyn. And those are my parents, Bev and Perry."

Bev held on to Perry's right arm as they walked. Watching her family from a distance, Julie felt a sudden lump in her throat. "Last but not least is my aunt, Bonnie. She's my dad's sister. I'm surprised she remembered it's Christmas Eve. She forgets everything."

Julie glanced at Gwen. A fresh tear spilled down Gwen's left cheek. "They all sound so great. You're really lucky."

Julie smiled and risked placing her hand on Gwen's back. "Want to come with me to the service? It'll be short."

"I don't know." Gwen stared into her mug for a long moment, mulling the offer. "Maybe in a minute. Can I finish this?"

"Of course! Take your time."

"Don't wait on me."

"It's okay, I don't mind." Julie was wary of leaving Gwen alone again in her fragile state. But judging by Gwen's expression, Julie feared pressuring her too much. She had not expected Gwen to be open to her invitation.

"No, you go ahead."

"Okay, well, when you're ready," Julie pointed out the window, "the courthouse square is just a few blocks down the street to the left." She unlocked the café's front door. "I'll see you there, okay?"

* * *

Light snow continued falling as Pastor Tim stood on the courthouse steps and read the Christmas story from the second chapter of the gospel of Luke. A small chorus of volunteers from three Cedar Springs churches stood on the steps behind Pastor Tim as he read.

Julie accepted a candle from one of the eager boys distributing them to the small gathering. Then she slipped past several townsfolk to join her family who stood near Beth and Eric. Everyone in the crowd held a small, lit candle. Perry tilted his candle toward Julie's so she could light her own, and as she did, she said a silent prayer of thanks that her dad was with them for Christmas after his heart attack scare.

* * *

Though full of apprehension, Gwen felt inexplicably drawn to join Julie at the candlelight gathering. She savored the last drop of the best hot cocoa she ever tasted, licked the inside rim of the mug, and set it down on one of the café tables. Then she exited Shelly's with one blanket still wrapped around her shoulders and walked cautiously down Main Street toward the courthouse square.

She arrived in time to hear Pastor Tim conclude his reading of the Biblical passage from Luke: "*And this shall be a sign unto you; Ye shall find the babe wrapped in swaddling clothes, lying in a manger. And suddenly there was with the angel a multitude of the heavenly host praising God, and saying, Glory to God in the highest, and on earth peace, good will toward men.*"

Gwen stood near the Christmas tree, just behind the huddled crowd. She soon spotted Julie standing between Perry and Bev. But nagging insecurity and unworthiness clawed at her heart and she could not bring herself to approach them. Instead, she remained rooted to her spot beyond the crowd.

"So why Christmas? What does it really mean?" continued Pastor Tim. "We find a clear explanation in the third chapter of John: *For God so loved the world, that he gave his only begotten son, that whosoever believeth in him should not perish, but have everlasting life.* And later, in John chapter ten, Jesus says, '*I am come that they might have life, and that they might have it more abundantly.*' Christ is the greatest gift."

The chorus began singing "O, Holy Night" and the crowd promptly joined in. Gwen's eyes stayed locked on Julie and her family. She saw Julie put her arm around Bev, embracing her from the side as they sang. That kind of affection seemed foreign and unattainable to Gwen, yet she desperately longed to experience it.

As the song ended, Julie glanced around, searching for Gwen in the crowd. She suddenly worried about leaving Gwen alone at the café. She had not wanted to pressure Gwen into joining her at the service, but now thought perhaps she *should* have stayed with her. Julie felt a wave of panic until she finally spotted Gwen at the back of the crowd standing alone by the Christmas tree. She motioned for Gwen to join her, but Gwen looked away and stayed put, holding tight to the blanket around her shoulders.

Julie was about to approach Gwen when Mike stepped out from the crowd and whispered something to Pastor Tim. Tim nodded, and Mike proceeded to address the crowd.

"Excuse me for a moment everyone," began Mike, grinning. "In the spirit of the holiday, I just have a quick announcement I wanted to share. As most of you are probably aware, Ms. Harriet Paddock's house burned down and she lost everything. She's still recuperating in the hospital."

Julie's pulse quickened as Mike spoke. She had not talked with Mike since their regrettable interaction after their last court appearance and had no idea what he was about to share.

Mike continued, "Just a little while ago, Judge Goodrich called to let me know that due to an incredibly generous gesture by our friend Julie Shelly, Harriet is dropping the lawsuit effective immediately. The judge is rescinding the injunction. The lights will be back on for Christmas!"

The Shelly family looked at each other with wide-eyed, stunned expressions. Julie immediately hugged her parents as the crowd cheered. Beth, Eric, Hugh, Robyn, Bonnie, Teresa, and dozens of well-wishers descended on Julie with hugs and handshakes.

Mike embraced Julie and leaned close to her ear so she could hear him over the din of the crowd. "You might want to go ahead and pack those extra bags too. Because your full trip's back on."

Julie looked completely confused. "What do you mean?"

"Let's just say I've also been on the phone with our friend Sandy Wilson, and she said to tell you she's got you covered."

Julie was astonished and speechless, but Mackenzie and the other teenaged Van-sledding enthusiasts filled the void, stepping in to hug her. Marie and the rest of the Congolese families followed close behind with more congratulations. Overwhelmed, Julie beamed, her heart nearly bursting with gratitude.

From her removed perch, Gwen took in the exuberant scene. She was rather mesmerized by Julie's steadfast smile and natural, unfussy beauty. Gwen finally ventured a couple of steps closer to Julie and her family. She was close enough to be within earshot, but still far enough back to remain unnoticed thanks to the celebration engulfing Julie. She ascertained a radiance about Julie that seemed to draw in the family, friends, and acquaintances surrounding her. It seemed clear to Gwen people simply loved being around Julie. The jubilation almost made Gwen smile; yet the utterly lonely, frightened feelings retained their firm grip on her.

Gwen suddenly felt a deep and familiar pain, longing to be part of Julie's inner circle like the people she observed. But it felt almost as if she was watching them through the glass of her own prison cell. She thought of the bridge again, her stepdad's crashed truck, the unwanted baby inside her, and the dark, flowing water—all so many nooses around her neck. She wondered how she could experience this joyful tableau and go back to her grim reality. This was nothing more than a glorious mirage. She did not belong there and could not wriggle free of the thought that *maybe stepping off that ledge was the best option.*

A man stood beside Gwen, interrupting her torturous thoughts. She did not notice him approach. Startled, she glanced up at him. He wore a plaid shirt under a denim coat with wool lining, and a red plaid hunting cap with the flaps that covered his ears. He smiled warmly as he too enjoyed observing Julie's celebration.

Gwen resumed gazing at Julie, wondering if Julie forgot about her.

"Don't worry," the man began, "she hasn't forgotten about you."

Gwen glanced at him, her paranoia fully engaged.

"Have you ever seen anyone so loved?" asked the man.

She was disconcerted by the man's random question and felt embarrassed for blatantly gawking at Julie's interactions. She supposed his question was innocent enough, however, and her answer was easy.

"No," she replied.

"Want to know the secret? Very few people love others like Julie does. She's always there for everyone," continued the man. "Perry and Bev Shelly did a magnificent job raising her. Did you know she was adopted?"

Gwen did not know what to make of the curious man. Finally, she shook her head and said, "No."

"She was indeed. See that couple talking to her?"

Gwen looked back at Julie conversing with a gray-haired man and woman who were holding hands.

"They're the Mitchells," explained the man. "They help families, like Julie's parents, foster and adopt children. That's how Julie's parents found her. You might look them up when you get home." He held out a *Lighthouse Adoption Network* business card. "They can help."

Gwen hesitantly accepted the card from the stranger and examined it, though her mind spun with confusion. *Who was this man?* She was on the verge of running away from him. Slowly, she slid the card into her front jeans pocket. As she vacillated, he continued in his laidback, grandfatherly manner, "Yes, Julie has been blessing the people of this town her whole life. You know she gave Harriet Paddock almost all her savings? Harriet doesn't have a single friend in the world. I bet she does now though." He chuckled at the thought.

Gwen wondered how she might slip away and rejoin Julie. The evening had been unusual enough already, so she mustered bluntness she would not normally exercise with strangers and asked, "Why are you telling me all this?"

"Because you're an unusually blessed young woman, Gwen."

Gwen felt an instant tingling on the back of her neck and weak with fright. Knots in her stomach tightened the same way they did when her stepdad was about to strike her. She wondered how this man could possibly know her name. She had not spoken to anyone that night other than Julie. She took a stumbling step backward in the snow and managed to squeeze out, "How do you know my name?"

The man's hands remained in his coat pockets and he was nonchalant about her question, even seeming to expect it. He grinned. "Very few people get the opportunity you have tonight," he replied with an intriguing, reassuring tone.

Perturbed by the man's cryptic statement, she asked, "Opportunity for what?"

"The chance to glimpse their unborn child...all grown up." The man smiled heartily at Gwen, then turned his gaze toward Julie, who was still laughing with her family and Beth and Eric. The man looked back at Gwen, still smiling, though his brow furrowed a bit when he saw the terror in Gwen's eyes. "Don't be afraid, Gwen."

Gwen backed away slowly, her mind a muddled blur. She tripped on a fire hydrant behind her and fell onto her side in the snow. The man stepped toward her, offering his hand to help, but she refused it.

"Who are you?" she demanded, picking herself up as quickly as she could and forgetting Julie's blanket that now lay on the ground. The snow stung her exposed skin through one of the holes in the knees of her jeans.

"I'm an angel of the Lord." The man paused to gauge her expression, which was still quite terrified.

Gwen's practical, survival instincts suppressed any curiosity that lingered, and shaking her head vigorously, she began walking away.

"Gwen, don't be frightened." The man took a few quick steps after her, before stopping and calling out, "I know all about you…your mother in prison…your pregnancy…how you got that bruise over your eye."

Gwen stopped in her tracks. Stunned, she turned to face the man again. In a non-threatening manner, the man walked briskly to her.

"You took your stepfather's truck without him knowing, a 1972 Chevrolet Cheyenne, light-blue and white. You just started driving without a destination. All the while thinking about how you might get rid of your baby…and even end your own life."

As tears filled her eyes again, he smiled to reassure her. *"There is a way that seems right to a person, but its end is the way to death.* I came to show you a better way."

Gwen desperately wanted to believe the man. But this was far too incredible.

"You've been given a very rare glimpse, because God loves you, Gwen. He wants you *and* your daughter to live. Your baby grows up to be *Julie.*"

Gwen stared intently at the man through her tears. She could not deny his conviction. He was so calm and peaceful—certainly nothing seemed strange about him. She glanced past him at Julie, who was embracing Pastor Tim and Maggie.

Gwen shook her head again, returning to reality. "How? I mean…I don't believe it."

"I understand. I know all about the haze that shrouds human faith. But that doesn't make this any less true."

Gwen stepped past the man, staring in wonder again at Julie. Another possibility suddenly occurred to her and she asked him, "Am I dreaming?"

"Have you ever felt the sting of the wind on your face, or the snow on your hands like this in a dream? Or tasted hot cocoa like you had earlier?"

Gwen finally managed a slight grin and shook her head. They stood together and watched Julie for another moment. Then he pulled a card and envelope from his coat pocket.

"Here you go. In case you want to drop Julie a line sometime." He handed her the card and she examined it…. A Christmas card with a photograph on the front of the Cedar Springs bridge covered in Christmas lights.

"Just drop it in the mail," he continued. "The postal service will handle the rest. Their timing is impeccable." He winked at Gwen.

The chorus-led carol singing continued in the square. Now that Gwen was coming around to actually believe the stranger, she could not take her eyes off Julie.

"She's so beautiful. Can I stay here awhile longer?"

"It *is* just a glimpse. Besides, you must get started *living*."

Gwen looked into his eyes. The angel's smile was beyond comforting. She picked up Julie's blanket from the snow
and together, they turned from the crowd and walked back toward Main Street.

✳ ✳ ✳

In the pandemonium surrounding her after Mike's announcement, Julie was distracted from her concern over Gwen's
whereabouts. But as the singing concluded and the crowd slowly dispersed, she suddenly snapped back into focus and began
searching for Gwen.

"What's wrong?" asked Beth.

"Nothing. I'll tell you later," replied Julie. "I'll be right back."

Julie jogged through the snow across the courthouse square,
then up the sidewalk along Main Street, all the way to Shelly's.
She rushed inside the silent café and called out, "Gwen?"

The café was deserted. She noticed Gwen's empty mug on
the table, with the blankets she'd given Gwen draped over the
back of a chair.

Julie rushed back out the front door and resumed jogging
along Main Street toward the Cedar Springs bridge. Her mind
raced, primarily in dread Gwen might have returned to the bridge
and…tears stung her eyes at the possibility.

Panicked anew, Julie sprinted with every ounce of her
strength, the cold air scraping her lungs as she went. Snow fell
heavily now, but through the thick flakes she could just make
out the figure of a man standing on the side of the road ahead,
just before the bridge, near the entrance to the alcove where she
parked earlier. She ran until she reached him, and the moment
she saw his denim coat, plaid cap, and friendly face, she rec-

ognized him as the man she chased through the park. The realization astounded her, and in her shortness of breath she only
managed to utter, "Hey, it's *you* again!"

"Yes, I suppose it is," he said, amused.

"Do I know you somehow?"

"Not really. But I know who you are, Julie."

Her eyes narrowed at him. This was odd, yet entirely on par
with her recent life. "I'm not sure whether to be freaked out, or…"

"Don't be freaked out. I'm an angel of the Lord."

"I shouldn't believe you," she said, "but so many strange
things have happened lately that…somehow, I mostly do."

"Well, I do find that laying some groundwork first makes
my job a bit easier."

"But, if I'm allowed to ask, why did you run away
from me that day?"

"It wasn't quite time yet."

"Time for what? Sorry—I have *so* many questions."

"I'm sure you do."

"So I'm not crazy? All these random connections to the
movie and everything were on purpose?"

"They were indeed on purpose. We needed to get your attention in order for you to be here tonight. And no, you are not
crazy…not any more so than the rest of humanity."

"So are you, like, my Clarence?"

"Not exactly."

"Oh." Julie was slightly disappointed and still quite puzzled. "I'm sorry, I could just really use some clarification. The
past month has been totally confusing. I guess I thought all this
had something to do with me at first. Then I thought it must

be about Harriet. Then I found Gwen on the bridge tonight. *What* is going on?"

"You were right, Julie. All this *has* been about you…in a sense. Someone else needed to see what life would be like if you were born…" He turned to his right and nodded toward the bridge.

Julie followed his gaze. Brushing snowflakes from her eyes, she could barely see Gwen through the heavy snow, walking toward her crashed truck. "Gwen?"

"She is your mother."

Julie stared at him, profoundly awed in a way she had never felt in her life and would never feel again. Her knees felt weak and almost buckled. He nodded again, urging her forward. Hesitantly, she started toward the bridge and called out, "Gwen!" She looked over her shoulder at the angel, "Can she hear me?"

He nodded.

Julie felt a surge of vitality back in her legs and she ran across the bridge toward Gwen.

"Gwen! Wait!"

Gwen did not hear Julie at first and was almost to her truck. Julie ran harder and when she reached the middle of the bridge, suddenly realized it was no longer snowing heavily over her, like she was under a covering. She glanced over her shoulder at a remarkable sight: heavy snow continued falling on the half of the bridge she already crossed, and then it abruptly stopped, as if hitting a wall. On Gwen's half of the bridge, the air was freezing and still, but it was not snowing.

"Gwen!" Julie called again. This time, Gwen heard, stopped, and turned around. Julie ran the short rest of the way to her. Their eyes were already filled with tears as they stood face to face. They studied each other for a long moment, marveling at the occasion, then laughed nervously, even as their tears flowed.

Finally, Julie said, "I've always wondered what you look like."

They embraced and held tightly to each other.

"You're a miracle," said Gwen.

"So are you. Please don't forget that," replied Julie.

"I wish I could stay."

"Everything will be okay."

"I know. *Now* I know. Thank you." Gwen kissed Julie on the cheek, then finally let her go. "Goodbye, Julie."

"Bye."

Gwen continued to her truck and got in. After a brief fussing sound, the truck started, and she slowly backed out. Julie winced as the front fender noisily separated from the cedar tree. And yet, as Gwen turned the truck around in the road, Julie noticed the truck did not even have a scratch.

Julie watched Gwen drive away into the hallowed night, somehow back into 1986. She lingered even after the truck rounded the bend out of sight. Finally, she turned and walked across the bridge toward town, back into the heavy falling snow, smiling with every step. She paused at the end of the bridge where the angel had stood. She looked in every direction for him. But he was no longer there. She was alone in the street.

Julie slid her hands into her coat pockets and walked along Main Street, back toward Shelly's Boulangerie & Café. As she proceeded, the family's Christmas lights suddenly came on, block by block, until all of downtown Cedar Springs was brilliantly aglow once again.

Julie walked slowly, savoring the cold night air, the ample snowflakes, and every miraculous moment of that wondrous Christmas Eve. Her heart filled to overflowing, in awe of God's miraculous gift.

Chapter 25

Julie wanted to tell her family, and Beth, and anyone who would listen, all about her remarkable Christmas Eve. Instead, once she made it back to the quiet of her apartment over the garage, she pulled out her *Moleskine* notebook and wrote down every single detail about Gwen, the angel, and their stupefying interactions. She had to get it all down on paper before she forgot any part of it. She wanted to be able to remember every minute detail of that night for the rest of her life.

On Christmas morning, after the family opened presents, Julie relayed what happened the night before. She was hesitant at first, concerned about what they might think, but she explained everything in such vivid detail and with such conviction, that she quickly assuaged any skepticism. When Julie's narrative concluded, everyone was rather speechless. Finally, Perry ventured that a prayer of thanksgiving seemed the only appropriate response to such a miracle. So, the family bowed their heads and Perry thanked God for the gift of life through Jesus Christ, and for His wonders with human beings.

Later in the day, Julie recalled Mike's stunning news at the Christmas Eve candlelight service that Sandy Wilson was going to "cover" Julie's donation to Harriet. But Julie never expected Sandy to follow through so soon. That evening, Julie received an email from Sandy announcing the money transfer was already complete in the amount of $50,000—five thousand dollars *more* than Julie gave away. The gesture humbled Julie. She thought the amount was excessive, yet she knew Sandy could never be talked out of it.

✳ ✳ ✳

The morning after Christmas Day, Hugh helped Julie load her car, then they drove to Shelly's, where Perry, Bev, Bonnie, Robyn, Beth, and Eric poured out the back door to bid farewell to Julie. Teresa said her goodbyes first so she could return inside to cover the counter.

Julie could barely speak with the crippling lump in her throat as she hugged everyone goodbye. This was it—after years of talking and dreaming about it, she was actually leaving her family, and the SB&C, and Cedar Springs, for an entire year. It was a bizarre feeling.

Bev put on her customary brave face, though Julie could see the tears forming in her mom's eyes. Bev tried to cover her emotion with, "Did you remember your toothbrush?"

"Yes, Mom."

"Got your passport?" asked Perry, trying to sound upbeat, though red eyes betrayed his sadness as well.

"Got it, Dad."

"How 'bout an umbrella? I heard it rains in England all the time," offered Aunt Bonnie.

"I've got that too."

"Did you remember your new camera?" joked Beth.

Julie just gave her a look. *As if she could possibly forget that.*

"She'll send you all postcards," said Hugh as he opened the driver's side door of the car. "But we better get going before she misses this flight she's been planning her whole life."

Suddenly, a jeep surged into the parking lot, skidding a bit as it lunged to a desperate stop and the driver's side door flew open. Van clamored out of the vehicle, one arm tangled in the seatbelt, and yelled, "Wait!" He scrambled toward Julie, nearly losing his footing on an icy patch in the process.

Julie was shocked to see him, but she instantly knew that the window of opportunity had flung back open. "I need to tell you something."

"What?" he asked, with alarm in his eyes.

"I love you," she blurted.

The alarm in his eyes dissolved to relief, then to utter joy. "I love you too!"

"I thought you were going to your parents for Christmas," she said.

"I did. But then I drove all night to make it back in time."

"In time for what?"

Van glanced around at Julie's family, Beth, and Eric. He swallowed hard and clamped his hands together. "Well, I've been doing a lot of thinking."

The excited surprise on Julie's face faded into slight confusion.

He smiled at her and put his right hand in the front pocket of his coat. He took a deep breath before continuing. "Please know that I completely support your trip, and this is in no way an attempt to keep you from going. But I was just wondering if…" He knelt on one knee in the icy slush of the parking lot, pulled his right hand out of his coat pocket, and extended a small diamond ring toward Julie. "When you get back…will you marry me?"

Everyone's eyes turned to Julie in anticipation, but she was frozen speechless for a moment. Van filled the silent interim with, "I know it's *so* last minute, but I figured I better propose before you go and meet some Euro-hunk."

Julie grinned. "Well, I'll have to think on it…"

Van's smile dropped. Beth looked momentarily horrified. Bev and Perry exchanged nervous glances. Julie looked skyward as if in deep thought. Van remained on one knee, paralyzed.

"Yes," she replied with a smile.

"Yes?" he confirmed, standing to face her.

"*Yes!*"

He slid the ring on her finger. Beth squealed and hopped up and down. Eric grinned and shook his head. Van pulled Julie into his arms and their lips met in a sterling debut kiss.

Still in Van's embrace, Julie laid her head on his shoulder and said, "By the way, thank you for the camera."

"How do you know it's from me?" he feigned.

"I just know."

Perry hugged Bev and kissed her cheek. Then everyone swarmed the newly engaged couple.

Finally, Hugh interrupted the commotion to remind Julie of the long drive they had to the Charlotte airport. Van asked Hugh if he might drive Julie instead. Hugh handed him the keys to Julie's car, clapped him on the back, and said, "Drive safe, bro!"

Everyone waved and yelled, "Bye" as Van and Julie drove away. Van turned onto Main Street, drove across the red bridge, and took them beyond Cedar Springs. Julie admired her new ring in the brilliant morning sunlight and reveled in all that was on the horizon.

It was a three-hour drive to Charlotte, and a good thing, because she had much to tell Van about her Christmas Eve.

✳ ✳ ✳

After more than an hour in the airport security line, Julie made it through the final checkpoint, tied her sneakers back on, and donned her oversized backpack.

She turned to her right out of the security bay, glancing up at the overhead gate number signs. Assured she was headed in the right direction, she proceeded down the concourse hallway toward her departure gate. In just over an hour she would be in the air, on her way to London. She quickened her pace, already exhausted, but exhilarated.

Gwen, now forty-eight years old and wearing her flight attendant uniform, pulled her compact, rolling suitcase behind her through the airport concourse. Julie and Gwen walked past each other, close enough to touch, headed in opposite directions.

They did not see each other, yet in the same moment they both smiled as their shared memory of that remarkable Christmas Eve simultaneously filled them with indescribable peace, joy, and deep gratitude for the gift of life.

About the Author

Nathan Nipper writes for television, radio, and online media at Mercury Radio Arts. He previously authored the independent nonfiction book *Dallas 'Til I Cry*, which won the 2014 MLS Book of the Year Reader's Choice Award from WorldSoccer-Talk.com. He is an American history buff and a soccer enthusiast who coaches his youngest son's team. He spent his childhood in Arkansas, later moving to France and Senegal where his parents served as missionaries. He is a graduate of Ouachita Baptist University and earned a master's degree in communication from Regent University. He lives in North Texas with his phenomenal wife, daughter, and two sons. *Life on Christmas Eve* is his first novel.

Connect with the author at **www.nathannipper.com.**